5861

5861

F
COR

Corcoran, Barbara

The potato kid

$13.95

DATE			
JAN 0 5 1992			
FEB 0 5 1992			
FEB 1 2 1992			
MAR 0 6 1992			
MAR 2 6 1992			
SEP 1 5 1992			
MAR 0 2 1993			
MAR 0 9 1995			

PL-97-35
CHAPTER 2

The Potato Kid

Books by Barbara Corcoran

A DANCE TO STILL MUSIC

THE LONG JOURNEY

MEET ME AT TAMERLAINE'S TOMB

A ROW OF TIGERS

SASHA, MY FRIEND

A TRICK OF LIGHT

THE WINDS OF TIME

ALL THE SUMMER VOICES

THE CLOWN

DON'T SLAM THE DOOR WHEN YOU GO

SAM

THIS IS A RECORDING

AXE-TIME, SWORD-TIME

CABIN IN THE SKY

THE FARAWAY ISLAND

MAKE NO SOUND

HEY, THAT'S MY SOUL YOU'RE STOMPING ON

"ME AND YOU AND A DOG NAMED BLUE"

RISING DAMP

YOU'RE ALLEGRO DEAD

A WATERY GRAVE

AUGUST, DIE SHE MUST

THE WOMAN IN YOUR LIFE

MYSTERY ON ICE

FACE THE MUSIC

A HORSE NAMED SKY

I AM THE UNIVERSE

THE HIDEAWAY

THE SKY IS FALLING

THE PRIVATE WAR OF LILLIAN ADAMS

THE POTATO KID

The Potato Kid

BARBARA CORCORAN

A Jean Karl Book

Atheneum   New York

To Julie Fallowfield,
for the professional care,
the friendship, and the laughter

Atheneum
Macmillan Publishing Company
866 Third Avenue, New York, NY 10022
Collier Macmillan Canada, Inc.
Printed in the United States of America
10 9 8 7 6 5 4 3

Library of Congress Cataloging-in-Publication Data
Corcoran, Barbara.
The potato kid/Barbara Corcoran.—1st ed. p.   cm.
"A Jean Karl book."
Summary: Fourteen-year-old Ellis thinks her summer is ruined when
her family takes in ten-year-old Lilac, a child from the potato country
of northern Maine.
ISBN 0–689–31589–9
[1. Summer—Fiction.] I. Title.
PZ7.C814Po 1989 [Fic]—dc20
89–14935 CIP AC

chapter 1

I was lying in the tall grass on the other side of the hedge that encloses our lawn and patio, watching an ant crawl up my arm. Summer had just begun, school was just out, and I was enjoying every minute of freedom. "If that was my sister Diantha's arm," I told the ant, "you'd hear an ear-cracking shriek, and you'd go flying through the air, and if she could find you, you'd be squashed flatter than an inkblot under her number-five triple-A spectator pumps." But of course Diantha would never be sprawled out in tall grass. It makes grass stains, and it wrinkles your dress or your designer jeans, as the case may be, and it gets your hair all out of sync.

But nothing could make my old cut-offs look any worse than they do, or my T-shirt with the faded picture of Einstein; and I have brown curly hair, cut short, that looks as if I never combed it, although I do. My father says my hair is most appropriate on Halloween.

I put the ant on the ground and sat up. I heard

Diantha's cultivated voice (she got an A in speech) and her friend Amalie's screechy giggle. My saturation point with eighteen-year-olds is low, but if I stood up to leave, they'd see me, and Diantha would say, "Oh, it's my little sister." She's only four years older, but you'd think it was a generation. Or she'd say, "It's only Ellis," like "It's only the garbage collector."

Well, I had something more important to think about than my sister. Just yesterday I had had an invitation to spend what was bound to be the best month of my life, the month of August, at the Equestrian Center in Massachusetts. I would only be a stable girl, mucking out stalls and carrying buckets of water and maybe once in a great while getting to exercise a horse, but just being around all those wonderful horses and riders would be heaven.

The way it happened was this: My best friend Maddie's father trains and sells polo ponies and saddle horses. He used to live in the town where the Equestrian Center is, but now he's sort of semi-retired here in Maine, because of an accident he had. He still buys and trades horses but not in such a big way. He has a friend, Mr. Blaise, who's in charge of the stable boys (and girls) at the Center, and Mr. Ryan asked if I could come there for a month to work around the stables. There's no pay except room and board, but who wants to get paid! Just being there would be enough. It took a lot of talking to persuade my mother, but my dad was on my side.

Maddie and I want to have a really good riding stable when we get through school. When I started riding lessons, way back before I even knew the

Ryans, my teacher said, "Ellis, I hate to tell y
but you're never going to win any blue ribbo
just don't have it. But you have a way with
You'd be good with a riding school or a sta____ _
that's when I mapped out my life. And it's really
okay with me. If I had to ride in a show, I'd probably
fall off the horse in nervous prostration.

So mucking out stables and grooming beautiful
horses was okay with me. For the last four summers
I'd worked for Mr. Ryan doing that kind of thing,
but this year I gave the job to my kid brother because
he wanted it so much. He might turn out to be the
one who gets the blue ribbons. He rides like a dream.

It would have been perfect if Maddie could go
to the Center, too, but summer is her father's busy
time, what with the polo teams he's started and all
that, so she was needed at home.

Amalie's shrill voice pierced my daydreams.
"Honestly, Di," she was saying, "you got robbed.
With your looks and your talent, you should have
been Miss South High, not runner-up. That Molly
Howe isn't even pretty. You could have gone on to
be Miss Maine, and a model or a movie star. Who
knows what you might have risen to."

Yeah, who knows what: Miss Milky Way, Miss
Universe? Diantha had just come in second in the
city high school's beauty and talent contest. She'd
played *To a Wild Rose* on her violin. It brought tears
to my mother's big blue eyes. To my brown ones, too,
but from a different emotion.

Diantha laughed the lilting laugh that it took
her a year and a half to perfect. "You're prejudiced,
Am. Because you're my friend."

3

Diantha always explains the obvious.

"No, it really wasn't fair," Amalie said.

It kills me when people talk about life being unfair, as if some big judge sits at a bench making these decisions about our lives. Important questions like: Will or will not Bobby Ames ask me to go to the Dairy Queen? When they say Life, do they mean God? If so, why don't they say so? I think it's a bum rap to blame life or God or tarot cards for what happens to you. Like I tell my kid brother, Jay, "You're on your own, bozo."

I crawled away from the patio until I could stand up without being seen by my sister. If they saw me, Amalie would be sure to say, "Ellis, you're getting so *tall!*"

I got my bike and rode past the new Volvo—that would be Myra French—and the '87 Buick—Frances Horton—the '78 Mercedes that Mona Harrod always pointed out was a Real Antique, and the huge station wagon in which Ruth Dawes brought the rest of my mother's bridge club. It was always wise to stay away when the club met at our house, unless you wanted to hear eight high voices trying to outtalk each other.

My brother usually lurked in the kitchen to snatch the remains of the sandwiches and hors d'oeuvres, but I noticed his bike was gone. He was probably over at the Ryans'. Part of his new job was going to be walking the horses at the polo games, and he could hardly wait for the first game.

I cut around the corner and down an alley, heading for the Ryans'. Maddie has been my best friend since fourth grade. My mother turns up her nose

4

because the Ryans are Irish and Italian Catholics, and she claims Mr. Ryan always smells horsey. My mother knows it's not nice to sound bigoted, so she tries to find other reasons why I should enlarge my circle of friends.

Maddie's mother is Italian, and I think she turns her nose up at us as much as my mother does at the Ryans. It's crazy when you think about it. All of us, including the Pilgrims, are immigrants or descended from immigrants, except Native Americans, and if you want to go back far enough, they came from Asia. But it's not the kind of thing you can have a rational discussion about with people like my mother. Who is okay in lots of ways but not that one. The way I finally won her over on letting me go to the Equestrian Center was to tell her that Princess Anne and Prince Philip have ridden there.

I was turning into Maddie's street when a screech of bike tires right behind me made me swerve. It was my brother.

"Why aren't you home snuffling out the eclairs?" I said.

Just then the Episcopal rector beeped his horn and waved.

"That's why," Jay said. "Father Seth never leaves a crumb."

"How do you know he's going to our house? The bridge club is meeting."

"It isn't the bridge club, stupid. It's the Women's Guild. The annual meeting of the DO-GOOD committee. They've got to think up a new project. Do you think Mr. Ryan will let me take Tempest down to the polo field for a run?"

"Sure." Jay would make a good jockey. He's a wiry little guy with muscles that he spends a lot of time on. After school let out, he went and got his hair cut so short he looked scalped. My mother nearly fainted when she saw him. He has big brown eyes with long lashes, but anybody that kids him about his gorgeous eyes had better say it and run; he's not shy about using those muscles. Also it is not wise to mention his 180 IQ. I consider him my best friend, even over Maddie.

We rode into the Ryans' yard, and Jay went straight to the stable. The Ryans have a big old house that needs paint, but Mr. Ryan never gets around to it, and Maddie's older brother, Cy, spends all his time in the shed with his computers. So nobody rakes leaves or cuts the grass till it's knee-high, and then Mr. Ryan cuts it with a scythe, swinging away like Father Time.

The doorbell hasn't worked for years, so I knocked on the frame of the screen door and shaded my eyes to look into the hall. Maddie's mother came to the door. She is what my father calls a fine woman, but I think he's as scared of her as I am. She is about a foot taller than her husband, and broad in the shoulders. She wears her black hair pulled back so tight it makes wrinkles in her skin, and she has coal-black eyes that glare at you as if you're some kind of bug to be stepped on. Then she'll startle you sometimes by bursting into loud laughter when you don't know that you've said something funny. In our town, which is mostly old conservative Maine people, Mrs. Ryan really stands out.

"I was looking for Maddie," I said.

6

"I didn't think you were looking for me." She has a strong Italian accent, which makes things even more intimidating. "Have you tried the stable?"

"No, I haven't, but I will. Thank you. I'm sorry I bothered you. How are you feeling, Mrs. Ryan?" When I'm nervous, I chatter.

She looked me over from head to foot. "My health," she said, "it is always perfect."

I thanked her again and backed off the porch.

Maddie was in the stable, grooming Tex, my favorite horse, and Jay was already at work mucking out the stalls. I could hear the racket of the printer coming from the shed attached to the barn, where Cy had his computer. He works for himself, putting together software programs. Jay has explained to me about ten times what Cy does, but I don't know a Fortran from a floppy disk. Computers make me nervous.

"Hi, Ellis," Maddie said. "What's new?"

"Not a thing since I talked to you an hour ago," I said.

She pretended to take a swat at me with the grooming brush. "I suppose you want to ride Tex. Well, I got news for you, and you're going to hate it."

"What?"

"He's been sold. Dad sold him to Mrs. Hallowell's grandson."

"Oh, yuck," I said. Mrs. Hallowell is president of the Women's Guild. She was probably at our house right that minute. She is also very, very rich. My father is a CPA, and the Hallowells are his biggest account. But that grandson is a spoiled brat. "Then

7

who do I get to ride?" Luckily for Jay and me, Mr. Ryan always needs people to exercise his horses, and he gets us for free.

"You could ride Tempest if you want."

Tempest is a nice bay gelding, though, in spite of his name, not as spirited as Tex. But in the horse business you have to get used to seeing your favorites go to some client. And the Hallowells were good, steady clients.

Maddie washed her hands at the iron sink. I gave Tex a lump of sugar. "Don't let that Hallowell kid ride you too hard."

"They're good riders, all the Hallowells," Maddie said.

She was right. Old money, blue blood, a place like the Stately Homes of England, and expert horsemanship—that was the Hallowells. And a talent for getting other people to do their work. Right now Mrs. H. was probably thinking up things for the Guild members to do while she flew off to Europe. It happened every year.

We saddled up a couple of horses that needed exercise and rode off toward the woods, where there were some good bridle paths. We cantered up the sandy road, the sun on our backs, and I felt about as happy as I ever felt in my life.

We slowed to a walk in the woods. The pines smelled good, and my little bay mare had nice smooth gaits. "I'll keep a diary when I'm in Hamilton," I told Maddie.

She laughed. "You won't have time. Mr. Blaise will probably work you to death."

"I'll be there for the Rolex Show, and the Katherine B. Clarke Welcome Stakes. Think of it, Mad! The best horses from all over the world."

"The Rolex United States Equestrian Team Show-Jumping Talent Derby," Maddie said. "I always wondered how that would look on a T-shirt."

"I told my father the other night that I thought I'd go to horsemanship school instead of college."

"And he said?"

"'Not instead of. *After.*'"

Maddie laughed. "You'll never talk him out of that."

"Oh well, it's a long way off."

"When are you going out to the farm?"

"Maybe next week. It depends on how Granddad is feeling."

My grandparents still live on the little farm where my dad grew up, a few miles out in the country. My granddad owned a small shoe factory once, but he went broke when a big company moved in up the coast. So they don't have a whole lot of money— in fact, very little—but they don't seem to mind. They do a little farming and my grandmother makes and sells quilts. We all love them very much, and I love to go out there.

"I wish you could go with me."

"So do I," Maddie said, "but there's too much work to do here. Polo games getting started and all."

Her father started the polo club seven or eight years ago, and it has become a very popular sport in the area.

"Dad says maybe we can come down for the Rolex, though." Maddie was riding ahead of me, the sun shining on her dark hair. She is tall for her age and big-boned like her mother. Someday she'll be beautiful. I always wish I looked like her. I'll always be short, and I have small bones. I need a hand up when I mount a big horse.

"Well," I said, "it looks like the best summer of my life."

Later there were quite a few times when I remembered saying that.

chapter **2**

My mother always says she has one inflexible rule: Be on time for dinner or go without. And she means it. She hates to cook, so she figures if she's going to make the great sacrifice of feeding us, the least we can do is be there.

So we all converge on the dining room pretty much at the same time. That night Jay got there first, starving as usual; Diantha wandered in looking bored; I tripped coming downstairs and sort of lunged into the room; my father sauntered in with a bottle of Diet Coke in his hand. But there was no sign of my mother.

We all sat down, and Dad asked the usual questions about our day. Once in a while it occurred to me that we never asked him about his, but I don't suppose it would have been very interesting.

Dad looked at his watch.

"Where is Mother?" Diantha said. She is in a "food is so boring" phase. She toys with her meals, and then later if you time it right, you find her stuffing herself in the kitchen.

Jay got up and pushed the swinging door into the kitchen. He came back to the table. "She's talking on the phone, and I don't see any food."

"The Guild bunch were here today," I said. "Sometimes they stay forever, especially when they're on the DO-GOOD project."

Dad sighed. "Is it that time of year already? Seems like we just got through sending checks to Tents for the Homeless."

"I wonder if anybody on that committee ever spent a Maine winter in a tent," Jay said. "They think *poor* means not having enough money to air-condition your car."

My father pushed back his chair and got up. "I'm in the den if anybody wants me."

"I'm *starving*," Jay wailed. "Aren't we going to eat?"

"All things come to him who waits," Dad said.

"I may go into shock," Jay said. "My blood sugar is sinking."

At that moment my mother made one of her entrances. When she looks that triumphant, it's usually because she's talked somebody into something.

"Well!" she said. "It's going to work like a charm."

"What is?" Diantha said. "May I be excused?"

"Mama!" Jay grabbed her hand like a drowning person. "Food!"

"Oh, I'm afraid we'll have to eat out." She looked at Dad. "The committee didn't leave till after five, and I've been on the phone to Mother."

"Whose mother?" Dad said quickly.

"Darling, since I am the mother of everyone

here except you, and I certainly was not talking to myself, *your* mother." She made it sound jokey, but there's always a little undercurrent when they talk about Grandma. Dad thinks Mom patronizes his parents, and I think she does, too, but I don't think she knows she does. Her parents, who are dead, had quite a lot of money, and were much more sophisticated than Dad's family. I don't remember the Ellis grandparents, but I know they left each of us a trust fund for college.

"What were you talking to Mother about, not that it's any of my business," Dad said. "And if we're going out to dinner, let's go before Jay collapses."

We went to the Red Lobster, and even Diantha showed some interest. Me, I could eat my weight in lobster boiled in the shell with plenty of melted butter.

Mom hadn't answered Dad's question, but you could tell she was bursting with some kind of news. When we were eating our clam chowder, she said, "We had a very exciting meeting today. Mrs. Hallowell had the most riveting idea for our annual project."

"Sandra Hallowell as a riveting woman is a concept that never occurred to me," my father said.

"John." My mother looked around to see if anyone heard him. In St. John's parish you don't joke about Mrs. Hallowell. She may not literally tithe, but she contributes a bunch of money.

We waited while the waitress brought food.

"What was her idea?" Diantha asked.

"She has just come back from her lodge up in the north—"

"Lumber," Dad said. "That's where old Francis Hallowell made his fortune."

"Anyway," my mother said, "she says the poverty in that part of the state is appalling. People with potato farms that aren't bringing in any money, out-of-work loggers—"

"Those are different areas," Dad said. He likes things to be said precisely. "Potato country is east and south of the logging country."

My mother said with exaggerated patience, "*Anyway,* those people are suffering. Most families have eight or ten children, and not enough to eat. . . ."

"That's awful," Diantha said. "Why doesn't somebody do something?"

"Somebody is," my mother said triumphantly. "*We* are."

Dad looked suspicious. "What is the Guild up to now?"

My mother put her hands flat on the table. Her diamond ring sparkled. "This summer several of us on the DO-GOOD Committee are each going to be responsible for one child. It's Christian love at the grass-roots level." She beamed at us.

I froze with a lobster claw halfway to my mouth. Jay stopped chewing his fried oysters, and Diantha turned pale. In a tight voice she said, "Mother, if you think you're going to dump some wild north-woods brat on us for the summer—"

"Wait a minute," Dad said. "Let's get this straight." He put down his fork. "Just what do you have in mind, Muriel?"

Mom was beginning to look nervous. "It's not

what *I* have in mind. It's Mrs. Hallowell's project, and naturally we were all for it." She didn't have to remind him that the Hallowells were his biggest account.

But he wasn't going down without a fight. "And you called my mother. For what reason, if I may ask?"

"Well, obviously, we can't take on a child. I'm committed to working in the church thrift shop three days a week this summer. Diantha has reading to do for college. And Ellis will be going off to that horse place. Myra is taking hers up to their cottage at Northwest Harbor, and Merle is sending hers to Girl Scout Camp with her own children. Since we don't have a summer cottage . . ." She gave Dad a reproachful look. "But there are your parents on that nice little farm just ten miles from here. This child could be such a help to them. And our children will go and help out when they can."

"Not me," Diantha said. "I'm booked solid for the summer. I've got books a yard high to read for that lit course."

"If it's for all summer," I said, "I'll be gone in August."

"And you bullied Mother into saying yes," Dad said. "Muriel, Dad is not well. They're old. They can't take on some unknown kid."

"Is it a boy or a girl?" Jay said.

"I have no idea." Mom was beginning to sound irked.

"Where do they come from? Who picks them out?" Diantha asked.

"It's a church project. Mrs. Hallowell talked to

the three churches in that town and arranged things with them."

"One's Episcopal, I suppose," Jay said.

"There is no Episcopal church there. I believe there is a Pentecostal and a Lutheran and . . . I really don't know. You are always telling me," she said to Dad, "that denomination makes no difference."

"I didn't ask that question; Jay did."

"I just wondered," Jay said.

"How many kids are the Hallowells taking?" Dad said.

"They're going to Italy for the summer."

"What a cop-out," I said. This whole plan was making me nervous. What if the grandparents found it was too much for them? Who would get stuck with the kid? "Don't forget," I said firmly, "I'll be gone in August."

"Who's paying for all this? Food, transportation, possible medical bills?" my father asked.

"Mrs. Hallowell is underwriting the whole project."

"Has anybody asked these kids if they want to do this?" Jay said. "Spending the summer with total strangers?"

Mom was beginning to look frazzled. "What do you want for dessert?" she said. She put on her gracious face for the waitress, who was standing beside us. "Do you recommend the peach pie?"

"It's real good." The waitress waited patiently while we all made up our minds. Diantha changed her order twice. Jay ordered a double portion of cheesecake with two kinds of ice cream.

When we finally started home, Dad said, "I'm going to have a talk with the folks about this. Dad has not been feeling well."

"I know that, dear." Mom patted his knee. "That's why I think this little person from up north can be such a help to them."

Later Jay and I rendezvoused behind the garage, which used to be a barn.

"What do you think?" he said.

"I think Mom's pretty slick the way she gets the credit for being a noble Christian, and other people do the work."

"Just so she doesn't count on me. I've got my job."

"She'd better not count on any of us. We're all busy."

"I wish I knew if it was a boy or a girl. It could be some real tough logger's kid that likes to beat people up."

"You'd better go down to the Y and take a few karate lessons." I gave him one of the licorice whips that I usually have in my pocket. It had a little lint on it, but he didn't care. "Whoever he or she is, that kid is probably more worried about the summer than we are." I lifted my licorice stick in a toast. "Here's to enriching experiences."

chapter 3

"How is this kid going to get here?" Jay asked. "U.P.S.?"

It was The Day.

"They're coming by Greyhound." Mom was trying to pretend she wasn't nervous. "One of the church people up there is bringing them. Some of them, anyway. Myra picked hers up on her way to Northwest Harbor, and I think Helen Brenner is taking hers off the bus at Bangor; they're going to their summer place at Blue Hill."

We were sitting on the front porch, all except Diantha, who had washed her hands of the whole affair. Maddie was there with her horse hitched to the porch railing, making my mother nervous. She's terrified of horses.

"Do you know yet if it's a boy or a girl?" Maddie said.

My mother shook her head and frowned as Maddie's horse took a mouthful of morning glory vine.

"If it's a boy and he's from logging country," Jay

said, "he can chop Grandpa's winter firewood."

"Actually," my mother said, "I believe the children are from potato farms."

"Potato farms!" Maddie burst out laughing. "Maybe it's a couch potato. Set it in front of the TV and forget about it."

"There isn't any TV at the farm," I said. "Granddad thinks TV is destroying the human race."

"Poor Granddad," Jay said. "I don't know why he has to get stuck with this kid."

"Then you do it," Mom snapped. She was getting pretty tired of our comments. "Ellis, you can go to the farm with the child for the first few days, to get him or her acclimated."

"Oh, sure." I couldn't believe Mom hadn't even bothered to find out what sex this kid was. Or how old. Grandma is a wonderful sport about things, but she has arthritis now, and it isn't easy for her to do things. You could hardly expect her to play softball or whatever kids in potato country play.

Mom looked at her watch for the tenth time. "We'd better go." She went into the hall and looked in the mirror, patting her hair. In spite of the way she acts so poised, my mother has a mile-wide streak of insecurity. She thinks she isn't pretty. But at her age, why worry? She's got a husband, she's popular in town. What's a slightly crooked nose and a few freckles?

I guess her mother was beautiful and glamorous. I'm not pretty either; I look like my mother, and it doesn't bother me a bit. (And if you believe that, you'll believe anything.) But we react differently: She checks herself out in the mirror all the time and worries about clothes and makeup. I try never to look in a mirror, and unless I'm forced to, I never dress up.

Maddie mounted her graceful little mare and rode along behind the station wagon until we finally got too far ahead of her. Jay was facing backward, watching Maddie's horse.

"That Miranda is a beaut," he said. "If Maddie let her out, she'd get to the bus station before us."

My mother shuddered. "People shouldn't ride horses downtown."

"Gramps remembers when horses was all there were," Jay said. "They and a whole squad of guys to clean up the horse . . . uh . . . manure. They called 'em white wings."

"Why?" I said.

"Because they wore white uniforms, stupid. Mom, you're going to get run in for obstructing traffic if you don't speed up a little."

"I don't need any backseat drivers," my mother said.

"You'd make a great hearse driver." Jay stretched out full-length on the backseat. "I hope this kid isn't a creep. He may carry a switchblade, you know."

"Jay!" my mother said. "Don't be absurd. Now, I want you to remember to be nice to this child. It's had a hard life, and it's our job to bring a little cheer into his life. Or hers."

When we pulled up at the bus station, the Bangor bus was sitting outside, empty. Nobody was around but a guy pushing a baggage cart.

"We missed her," I said. "Maybe she took the

bus back home." I felt immensely relieved.

"Don't be silly," Mom said. "They must be inside."

I could tell she was nervous, too. She scraped the curb with the tires when she parked.

Jay jumped out and ran into the terminal.

I said, "I'll wait here." I really didn't want to find any kid in there waiting for us. My summer was falling apart all around me.

My mother opened my door. "You will come with us."

It was the no-argument tone, so I got out and she locked up.

Jay came galloping back. "All I can see is three people, one woman and two kids, at the far end of the station. The woman is reading a *Reader's Digest*. The boy looks as if he's asleep. The other one is scrunched up in the seat, and I can't even see if it's a girl or a boy."

"*Two* of them?" My mother looked pale.

We went inside. The boy Jay had described was big and kind of fat, or maybe it was the heavy plaid shirt he was wearing. He had to be really sweating in that shirt. It was a hot day. His jeans were too small for him. They were faded, but not by Calvin Klein.

The woman was tall and thin with glasses. All I could see of the other kid was a pair of bare skinny legs and dirty white sneakers, no socks.

They hadn't seen us, and for a minute we stood there looking at them. "*Two* children?" Mom said again. "Surely not two."

Just then Mrs. Harrod came dashing in. I could

see her shiny old Mercedes double-parked near our car. "Muriel!" she cried. "Are they here?"

Mom looked relieved. "They must have arrived early. I suppose they're the ones over there. Nobody else is here. You'd think a big company like Greyhound could keep to their schedule."

"Well, let's move it," Jay said. He started toward the group.

The boy turned his head and saw us. His hair was so blond it was almost white, and he needed a haircut. He looked scared as he said something to the woman. She put down her magazine and stood up, looking relieved. The kid on the far side of her scrunched down in her chair as if she were trying to disappear. She didn't look at us. Somebody had cut her reddish-blond hair with dull scissors; it was all different lengths with a cowlick that stood straight up. Even so, you could tell it was a girl, and I wondered if she was our potato kid.

Jay had no doubts. He ran up to the boy and said, "Hi. I'm Jay Worthington. You can ride my bike part of the time if you want to. It's a twelve-speed. I got it for my birthday. Do you like horses?"

The boy just stared at him with pale eyes. He looked paralyzed with fear.

"I think the young man is mine, Jay dear," Mrs. Harrod said. She and Mom introduced themselves to the woman.

"Yours?" Jay looked crestfallen. He gave the other kid a scowling inspection.

"I asked for a boy on account of my own boys," Mrs. Harrod said. "What's your name, son?"

The boy's mouth opened but no sound came out.

Maybe he was a mute. How would Mrs. Harrod deal with *that*?

"Tell Mrs. Harrod your name, Henry," the woman said.

Instead, he pointed to the name tag almost hidden by the pocket flap of his shirt. Mrs. Harrod had to lean over to read it.

"Henry Pelletier. That's French, isn't it?" she said. "That's wonderful. You can help my Gerald with his French."

"I don't believe Henry speaks French," the woman said. She smiled for the first time. "It's quite a challenge to get him to speak English, until he gets to know you."

Mrs. Harrod looked alarmed. "There's no . . . uh . . . problem?" she asked in a low voice that we all could hear.

"Oh, no. Henry is just a little shy."

There was a small sound from the other kid, like a laugh that was choked back. I stood in front of her, but she didn't look up. She seemed to be about nine or ten or maybe a small eleven. I leaned down to read her name tag.

"Lilac Kingsmith," I said. "What a neat name."

She bit her lip and stared at her clenched hands. I couldn't tell if she was trying not to cry or was scared or mad or what.

"My name is Ellis Worthington. Ellis was my mother's maiden name. That's why I've got two names that are really last names." I wanted to say, "And if you're planning to make any wisecracks about it, don't." "We're going to my grandparents' farm tomorrow or the next day," I said, "you and me.

Jay is my brother. My grandparents' farm is probably not as big as your potato farm, but it's nice. Do you like horses?"

She looked at me for the first time, and I was really startled. Her eyes were different colors. One was gray and the other was light brown with gold flecks. Her genes must have played a trick on her. "I hate horses," she said.

"I guess that's where we differ." I sounded sharper than I meant to, and she raised her eyebrows as if it was funny that she had gotten my goat. A smart-ass kid we had here.

The woman was giving Mom and Mrs. Harrod information and telephone numbers in case they had any problems.

"Oh, we won't have any problems, will we, Henry?" Mrs. Harrod spoke brightly, but she didn't look quite so sure as she had. She's really a nice woman, on the whole, and I felt sorry for her. You'd think those big oafs, her sons, would have come along to help out.

"On your feet, Henry." Firmly, the woman boosted Henry up. It looked as if she were hoisting a dead weight. She picked up a big paper bag and handed it to him. "That's Henry's suitcase," she said to Mrs. Harrod. "You've got my telephone number and address, Henry. You can write to me if you want to."

Henry obviously did not want to go off with Mrs. Harrod. He looked pleadingly at the church woman.

"Oh, go *on,* Henry," Lilac Kingsmith said.

I got the idea she'd had it with Henry on the long trip down.

24

Mrs. Harrod got a grip of his elbow and started to propel him toward the door.

"See you around, Henry," Jay said. "Maybe we can go to the beach someday."

Mom smiled at him, and I knew she was pleased that he'd said something kind to Henry. Jay is better at that than I am.

"Is that your suitcase?" I said to Lilac Kingsmith. She had her feet firmly planted on a battered and scarred leather suitcase tied together with a piece of clothesline. "I'll carry it for you."

She stood up and grabbed it with both hands. "No, you won't."

"Suit yourself." Getting along with Lilac Kingsmith wasn't going to be any lead-pipe cinch. It was a good thing Grandma was a peacemaker.

"So long, Lilac," the lady said. "You have a nice summer now." She put out her hand as if to pat Lilac, but the kid shrank back. It really must have been a great bus ride. The woman said good-bye to my mother and headed rapidly for the ladies' room.

We started out, Lilac behind us half carrying, half dragging the suitcase. What did she have in that thing anyway—rocks?

Any silence among people upsets my mother, and she rushes in to fill it. "Do you and Henry come from the same town, Lilac?"

"No," Lilac said.

"What town are you from?" Jay asked. He knew the northern part of the state better than I did, because Dad had taken him on fishing trips to some of those big lakes. He'd even been to Campobello, where President Roosevelt lived.

"No town," Lilac said.

"Oh." My brother was stopped in his tracks for once.

My mother was subtly looking Lilac over. "We'll probably go up to the farm the day after tomorrow," she said. "I want to buy a few clothes for Ellis first. Jeans and shirts."

I knew what she was leading up to. If there was anything I didn't need, it was more jeans and shirts. And there it came: "Perhaps," she said as if it had just occurred to her, "we could get some for you, too. Clothes wear out fast on the farm."

"I got clothes," Lilac said.

I wondered how we were going to get her a haircut. Maybe if Jay got her down and sat on her and I went at her with the shears, we could at least improve on that moth-eaten mop she had now.

When Mom unlocked the door of the station wagon, Lilac looked it all over.

"You lucked out," I said. "If Mrs. Harrod had got you, you'd have had a vintage Mercedes. If it was Mrs. French, you'd have got the new Volvo. . . ."

Mom gave me a look. "There's nothing wrong with our wagon," she said. "Lilac, why don't you sit up front with me?"

But Lilac was already scrambling into the backseat, hauling her bulging suitcase after her. Jay and I sat on the middle seat.

Mom had to raise her voice to talk to Lilac. Our wagon is one of those long jobs. "We're so happy you could come to us this summer."

No reply.

Mom looked in the rearview mirror. I could see

she was feeling out of her depth. "You and Ellis will have a great time together." It was a good try, but it lacked conviction.

When we got to our house, I thought Lilac was going to refuse to go in. We're not rich; I guess we're what they call upper middle, at least when Dad has a good year. Our house is certainly not elegant, but it is big. It's an old Victorian three-story with gables, built by a Congregational minister with seven children. At least that's the story. Maybe to Lilac it looked impressive, I don't know. If she'd looked close, she'd have seen it had damaged shingles, rusted rain gutters, and scraggly bushes.

"Here we are," my mother said too brightly. "Help her with the bag, Jay."

But again Lilac was having none of that. She climbed over her suitcase and then pulled it out and lugged it up the steps to the front porch. There she looked at the hammock that we keep up all summer. "I can sleep here," she said.

My mother took a minute to smooth out her face. "Perhaps later, when the nights are warmer, when you aren't at the farm. Right now I have a nice comfortable guest room for you." She pointed upward. "The one where that dormer window is. I think you'll find it a cozy room."

"Does the door have a lock?" Lilac squinted up at the window.

Mom looked at me.

"Yes, it does," I said, giving her my best false smile. "You can lock us out, and we can lock you in."

She gave me a wild look, like a cornered rabbit.

"Only kidding," I said.

Mom took her firmly by the hand and escorted her into the house. Jay and I went behind the garage and looked at each other.

"It's going to be an interesting summer," he said.

"I'll be away."

"Not till the first of August, you won't. I'll be working. *All* summer. Happy landings, chum."

chapter 4

Lilac was in her room with the door shut. I went upstairs two or three times to see if she wanted to come down, but when I knocked, she said, "Go away." The last time I went, she didn't answer at all.

"Let her alone for a while," my mother said. "She probably wants to get settled. It's hard to go into a strange house."

Dad was out in the backyard getting the charcoal briquets going in the Webcor. He was going to barbecue steaks, and Mom was putting together one of her famous potato salads. "Peel the carrot sticks, dear," she told me. "And please try not to take half the carrot off with the peel."

"When do we eat?" Jay said for the tenth time. He was stacking up plates and silverware to carry out to the patio.

Diantha breezed in with her tennis racquet and that rosy glow that tells everybody she won.

"Straight sets, I suppose," I said.

"Not quite," she said. "But close enough. Amalie

needs to work on her serve. Has the child arrived?"

"She's in the guest room," Mom said, "settling in."

"Or something," I said.

"What's she like?" Diantha was washing her hands at the sink, getting in my way as usual. "Is she possible?"

My mother frowned at her. "Diantha, all children are possible."

"Obviously," I said.

"Well, not necessarily," Jay said. "There are miscarriages and—"

"Never *mind!*" my mother said. "If you can't carry on a normal conversation, leave the room."

"Here I go." Jay staggered out the back door, balancing the six plates. I held my breath, waiting for the crash, but he made it.

My father was just coming in. "You could have a great career as a busboy," he said to Jay. Now *he* had to wash his hands. "When do we meet our guest?"

"I wonder if she knows how to manage the shower," Mom said.

"I showed her," I said. We have one of those one-handle-for-everything showers. "I told her if she turned it clear left, she'd freeze to death, and if she turned it clear to the right, she'd scald herself to death."

"That must have encouraged her," Dad said.

"Diantha, get out the sauces, please," Mom said.

"I have to take a shower." Diantha disappeared before Mom could stop her. Diantha takes about five showers a day.

"The steaks go on the fire in fifteen minutes," my father called after her. "If you want one, be here." He turned on the radio to *All Things Considered*.

I finished the carrots and got the Worcestershire and the chutney, and the soy sauce for my brother, who is probably the only person in the United States who douses steak in soy sauce. He claims he was an Oriental in a previous life. Sometimes all he eats for lunch is a soup plate of tofu drowned in soy sauce. One year at the top of his Christmas list he wrote *samurai sword*. My brother is not your ordinary everyday twelve-year-old.

When everything was ready, I went upstairs to get Lilac. Dad had started the steaks, and they smelled wonderful. I wondered if Lilac would mind our having potato salad. Maybe a kid growing up on a potato farm got sick of potatoes the way they say someone working in a candy factory can't stand chocolate. I can't imagine that, but I could get sick of potatoes, except my mother's potato salad.

I knocked on Lilac's door. No answer. I said, "We're about ready to eat, Lilac. You want to come on down?"

No answer. I could hear Diantha singing in the shower in the other bathroom. Actually, she has quite a nice voice. She always sings a lot when she's won anything, like a tennis game, or when she gets an A in biology. After she came in second in the beauty contest, she didn't sing a note for several days.

I knocked again. It was so quiet in Lilac's room, I got the crazy feeling that she had stopped breathing. Maybe she had died. Maybe the shock of leaving home was too much for her. I said, "I'm coming in, Lilac, okay?" I turned the door handle slowly and opened the door just a crack. I didn't want to scare the poor kid. If she had really stopped breathing, though, I'd have to get Diantha out of the shower. She had passed her lifeguard exams, and she could resuscitate people.

"Lilac?" I couldn't see her anywhere. I pushed the door open and went in. There was nobody there! I looked in the closet and under the bed. Nobody.

The window facing the McLarens' house next door was wide open. My heart began choking me. I was so sure she had jumped out and killed herself, I was scared to look.

When I couldn't see her suitcase anywhere, either, I made myself look out the window. The clothesline that had tied her suitcase together was tied to a limb of the pine tree that grows right outside that room. You can climb out that window onto the tree and shinny down to the ground; I've done it a hundred times when my mother wasn't home. When I saw the clothesline, I thought she might have gone down that way. Then it came to me what she'd done: She'd probably lowered her suitcase down on the clothesline and climbed down the tree. I was mad. She'd scared me half to death, and she wasn't dead at all. She'd just sneaked off.

When I came out of her room, Diantha was just coming out of the bathroom with a towel wrapped around her head and another one around her chest. She was singing a Bob Dylan song, sliding into the notes the way he does. It drives me crazy. I said, "She's gone."

It took her a minute to come out of her dream world. "Who's gone?"

"The potato kid." I was already running downstairs to the kitchen. "Hold one steak," I yelled at my father. "There's no guest."

They all turned to look at me.

"What are you talking about?" Mom said. "Where's Lilac? She's going to have to learn to be prompt at meals, like the rest of us."

"She may be prompt," I said, "but not here."

Dad came in, holding the long fork he turns the steaks with. He was wearing his big corny apron that says FATHER KNOWS BEST. Jay stuffed an olive into his mouth.

"What's the matter?" my father said.

"She's probably feeling shy," Mom said. "I'll go talk to her. Poor little thing, so far from home."

"Mom, I'm trying to tell you. She's not there. She's gone on the lam."

"Speak English," my father said sharply. "What are you saying?"

"She's escaped."

"That's impossible," my mother said. "If she'd come downstairs, I'd have seen her."

"She went out the window, suitcase and all. There's nothing left but a yard of clothesline."

Jay was the only one who didn't look amazed. "I'll take a look around," he said, and went outside.

Diantha came downstairs, fluffing out her half-dried hair. "When do we eat? You were kidding, weren't you, about the child?"

I went out after Jay, leaving my parents to explain that Lilac's disappearance was for real. Halfway to the garage I met Jay. He shook his head.

"She's not in the loft or anyplace. But she can't go anyplace very fast lugging that big old suitcase."

"Maybe she hid the suitcase and plans to come back for it after dark."

"Why?"

"Why what?" I was feeling really upset. I certainly didn't want that kid on my hands, but I didn't want anything bad to happen to her either. She was just a little kid, even if she was a pain in the neck.

Dad came out of the house looking grim. He hates it when he's right in the middle of barbecuing and something happens. With his apron still on, he headed for the car, so Jay and I ran and got in.

"You better take your apron off," Jay said to him.

He looked down as if he'd forgotten he had it on, jerked it off, and threw it in the bushes. "Where in blazes could that kid have got to?"

"If I were you, I'd head for the bus station," Jay said.

Dad backed out of the yard fast and started down the road to town. "Crazy idea in the first place," he muttered. "Somebody ought to pack up those kids and ship them over to her highness in Italy, or wherever she is." He meant Mrs. Hallowell. "Has these brilliant ideas and dumps them on other people."

Jay and I didn't say anything. When Dad is mad, it's just as well not to get into it.

Because it was most people's dinnertime, there weren't many cars on the road. You could smell some of the barbecues as we drove by, and Jay was clutching his stomach. I was pretty hungry myself.

Jay half stood up. "There she is." He pointed up the road. Ahead of us, looking about twelve inches tall, Lilac was half walking, half staggering under the weight of the suitcase. It must have been really hard to carry without the clothesline to hold it together. She was using both hands.

"Don't yell at her, Dad," I said.

"I'm not a monster," he said in a tone I didn't want to argue with.

He drove past her and stopped. I got out of the car fast and went back to her. She stopped in her tracks, but though she looked tired out and the sweat was pouring down her face, leaving smudges, she was not about to give up.

"What you want?" she snarled at me.

"Lilac," I said, "come on back and have some supper."

"Don't want any."

Dad got out and approached us, Jay right behind him. He was making an effort to be nice, and I think the more closely he looked at her, the easier it was. She did look pathetic.

"Hi, Lilac," he said. "I'm Mr. Worthington."

She glared at him.

"I hope you won't run out on us without giving us a chance."

"I'm goin'," she said.

"You got bus money?" Jay is always practical.

"I'll get it."

Looking at her face, I figured she would, even if she had to hold up the 7 Eleven.

My father is quite tall, and Lilac was little, so he scooched down to her level and looked her in the face. "I'm cooking special steaks in your honor," he said. "They're this thick." He held up his thumb and forefinger.

"Oh, sure," Lilac said.

"It's the truth. I've been looking forward to meeting you. My parents live on a farm, you know, where you and Ellis will be going. They're looking forward to meeting you, too."

Don't overdo it, Dad, I thought.

"So they can put me to work," Lilac muttered. "Free labor."

My father's patience was beginning to slip. I could see the little place in his cheek that starts to throb. "You'll do some chores, just the way Ellis and Jay do, to help out. I don't think it will kill you, Lilac."

She kept her head down, looking up at him from under her eyebrows. "They'll beat me."

My father caught his breath. I almost laughed at the idea of Grandma and Granddad, the two kindest people on earth, beating anybody. But if she really believed that, I guessed it wasn't so funny.

"We don't beat people, Lilac." My dad's voice had gotten gentler. "Do they beat you at home?"

" 'Course not. But when you hire out to strangers, they beat you and starve you, like in *Oliver Twist*."

I thought, well, at least she's read a book.

Dad said, "Nobody will touch you. You're not hiring out. You're our guest for the summer. But if you're worried, I'll make a deal with you. Stay one week. If you don't like it one week from today, I'll buy your ticket home and pay you twenty-five dollars for your time here. We have two witnesses. When

36

we get home, I'll put it in writing. Is it a deal?" He straightened up.

She had to lean back to look up at him. She studied his face, frowning. "Can I lock the door to my room every night?"

"Certainly."

"How do I know you're not all in this together? You're all kin to each other."

"Lilac," he said. "I am hungry, and my steaks are going to burn up. Is it a deal or isn't it?"

"All right," she said. "One week."

In a fast motion that took us all by surprise, he scooped her up, suitcase and all, and put her in the backseat of the station wagon. She was too amazed to do more than sputter.

Before she could change her mind, he made a U-turn, and we were on our way home.

Mom had set everything out on the patio table. She gave Dad an inquiring look, but she acted as if nothing had happened. Lilac sat huddled on the retaining wall as far away from the rest of us as she could get. Yet she couldn't take her eyes off the food. I wondered when she had eaten last.

Dad finished cooking the steaks, and then he piled a plate with food and took it to Lilac. He pulled up one of the little tables for her. "Enjoy yourself," he said. "There's more where that came from."

She hesitated for about one minute and then she tore into the food as if she hadn't eaten for a week. But then, so did Jay.

The rest of us talked about the kind of stuff we always talk about: Mom told Dad that Julia Peterson's husband was going to run for town council; Dad told her about a new client he'd just gotten; Diantha talked about a boy she'd met at the tennis court; Jay and I swapped insults. Now and then Mom looked over at Lilac and smiled, as if to include her in the conversation, and Diantha made a couple of futile tries at talking to Lilac, but I don't think Lilac even heard them.

When her plate was empty, Dad refilled it. I never saw a kid eat so much, so fast. Finally, then, as soon as she was through, she picked up her suitcase, which she'd kept by her feet, and started into the house.

"Let Jay carry that for you, dear," Mom said.

"No," Lilac said.

I noticed one of her pockets was bulging, and I could see the top of a Parker House roll. She must have been worrying that she wouldn't get fed again.

"I changed you to the room across the hall from where you were," Mom said. "I thought you might like it better."

"Has it got a key?" Lilac said.

"It's in the door. I'll come and show you."

Lilac interrupted her. "I'll find it."

Jay and I exchanged looks. The room across the hall didn't have a tree she could escape by.

We heard her thumping her suitcase up the stairs.

"When does she go to the country?" Diantha said. "Soon, I hope."

"That's enough of that kind of talk," my father said.

Diantha looked surprised. He is almost never sharp with her.

To Mom he said in a low voice, "She thought

we were going to beat her. Like *Oliver Twist,* she said."

"Heavens!" Mom said. "Well, at least she's read some books."

I had thought the same thing, but hearing Mom say it made me think we were snobs. Why shouldn't the kid have read a book? She went to school, didn't she? For all we knew, she might have very literate parents who just happened to be poor. My father's college roommate grew up very poor, but his father had ten cats all named for characters in Shakespeare.

Dad finished his Diet Coke. "I hope," he said, "I do fervently hope that Madame Hallowell is having a wonderful time in Italy."

"I hope her gondola tips over," Jay said.

chapter 5

My mother never gets up till noon, and in summer Diantha sleeps late, too. Jay is up at the crack of dawn, and I am somewhere in between. When school is in session, Dad fixes our breakfast, but in summer it's every man for himself. Or, as Diantha would say, every person for his or her self.

When I came down to the kitchen the next morning, Lilac was finishing off some pancakes. "Hi," I said.

She said something with her mouth full. I guess it was "hi."

"You must have been up early to get pancakes. Did you have breakfast with Dad?"

She nodded. "He cooks good."

"Yes, he does. Does your father like to cook?"

"He's dead."

"Oh." Leave it to me to say the wrong thing. "Is your mom a good cook?" I had a horrible feeling she was going to say she was dead, too.

But she said, "She knows fifteen ways to cook potatoes."

"I bet she'll miss you."

"She had to get me away from the kids so I can amount to something. My father was real educated, but he never amounted to anything because he was always sick. She thinks the weather killed him."

"What kids?"

"She had four kids by her second husband, the twins and then a girl and then a boy, bing bing bing, every year. And her husband had two young kids. He's dead, too, the second husband. Just this spring. Got killed in a bar fight. Now she's going to marry Marvin, and I don't want any part of that. He hates me. She has to, though, to get help with all those kids. So she wanted to get me free of 'em. Davey's already gone. He's eighteen, the lucky dog."

I had never heard her talk so much. "How old were you when your dad died?"

"Six."

Six! I tried to think how I would have felt. I wanted to ask more questions, but her face had that closed-up look, as if she had said too much already. "Did Jay eat with you and Dad?"

"He ate earlier. He fixed me some toast."

So she'd had two breakfasts. If she waited for Diantha, she could make it three, only that one would probably only be Rye-Krisp and black coffee.

"Where did Jay go, did he say?"

"He went to ride a horse. He was wearing funny pants."

"Jodhpurs." He had new ones that he was very proud of.

"I never saw pants like those."

"He got them for his birthday. You want some more cereal?"

She held out a bowl. "He had on cute boots."

I wanted to laugh. She seemed impressed with old Jay in his riding clothes. "Do you have horses on your farm?"

" 'Course not. What would we do with horses? Anyway, we lost our farm to the bank."

"Where do you live, then?"

"We moved into the old Farr place. Been empty for years. It was full of mice and bats. Has a wood stove that works, though."

"Does your mother work somewhere?" I knew I shouldn't be asking such personal questions, but I was trying to imagine how she lived.

"With all those little kids?" She dove into the bowl of cereal, dripping milk off her spoon. "She works when it's potato-digging time. We all do."

"Kids and all?"

"Sure. They close school so we can."

"What a break!"

She gave me a withering look. "You ever dig potatoes?" She wiped the milk off her chin with her hand. "Does your sister go out with fellas?"

"Sure."

"Well, tell her to be careful. My cousin Mae got caught, and the guy split. Now she's got this baby to look after. They live with us."

"How old is she?"

"Fifteen."

I hoped the old Farr place had a lot of rooms. "You want some toast?" She had finished the cereal and was looking around expectantly.

"Sure. You got any more of that jam?" There was an empty raspberry-jam jar on the table. It had been nearly full yesterday.

42

"How about orange marmalade?"

"I never ate any."

I got out the special orange and grapefruit marmalade that Mom orders from Williams-Sonoma. She'd probably have a fit. Well, she could order some more. I didn't want to feel sorry for Lilac, but I was beginning to.

Diantha came trailing in, in her housecoat, looking sleepy.

"What are you doing up so early?" I said.

"Mom told me to take you guys downtown to get you some clothes. Hi, Lilac. I'm going to make an omelet. You want some?"

"Sure," Lilac said. "What kind of clothes?"

"I don't know. Whatever you want, I guess."

Lilac looked suspicious. "You're kidding me."

"No, she isn't," I said. "Mom hates to go shopping with us. We've been picking out our own clothes for years."

Diantha beat the eggs, yawning. She made the omelet and split it with Lilac. "You have interesting eyes," she said to her. "Different colors. I wish mine were."

Lilac reared back. "Anybody makes fun of my eyes, I punch 'em right in the snoot, and don't think I won't."

Diantha's own blue eyes came wide open. "I wasn't making fun. I admire them. If I'd had something unusual like that, I might have won the contest."

Lilac still looked suspicious. Kids had probably given her a hard time. Anything the least bit different, and they come down on you. They used to call me Porky when I was in my fat phase.

Knowing how long it takes Diantha to shower and dress and put on her makeup, I said, "I'm going to take Lilac over to Maddie's. We'll be back by the time you're ready."

When all of Lilac's food was gone, we left, leaving Diantha dreaming over her coffee. She'd been out with a Cornell freshman the night before, and I heard her come in around two. We'd have plenty of time to shoot the breeze with Maddie.

We don't have an extra bike, so we walked.

"What contest?" Lilac said.

It took me a minute to know what she was talking about. "Di was in the high school's beauty and talent contest. She lost."

"My mother won a loggers' beauty contest once."

I was baffled. "Was she a logger?"

She snorted. "Guys are loggers. They put on the contest. She said it was all downhill after that."

"What does that mean?"

"She got married. It was all right at first, until my dad got sick and lost his job and we moved back to Aroostook County, where my mom was from, and lived on the farm she grew up on. My dad wasn't any good at farming. He was a schoolteacher, only nobody needed one."

"What was the second husband like?"

"Horace? He was all right. Never done a day's work in his life. Hated potatoes."

"Will you live up there when you finish school?" It sounded like a terrible place to live.

"I'm never going back there."

I was really startled. "Never?"

"Never. I'm going to amount to something."

She was ten years old. Was she planning to
44

amount to something right away? Or was she planning to stay with us? I began to worry.

When we came up to the Ryans', Mrs. Ryan was sweeping the porch, swinging her broom as if dirt were an enemy that fought back.

"Who have you got there?" she said.

I introduced Lilac. Mrs. Ryan looked her over. Lilac backed away. Then Mrs. Ryan began to sweep again, ignoring us. I steered Lilac toward the stable. "That's Maddie's mother. She's kind of moody," I said.

Maddie came out, leading a chestnut with white front feet. "Hi," she said. "You must be Lilac."

Lilac was staring at the horse.

"Do you like horses?" Maddie asked.

The chestnut turned his head toward Maddie. He was a pretty horse with a long silky mane that flew up as he tossed his head. Lilac couldn't take her eyes off him. I didn't know whether she was scared or awed or what.

When Lilac didn't answer, Maddie put the horse in the paddock and invited us into the stable while she finished her work. I remembered Lilac saying she hated horses, but she hadn't seen any good ones. Maybe she'd change her mind. She came into the stable, sticking close to my heels.

"Is Jay riding?" I said.

"Yes. He took Tempest out."

Maddie's brother, Cy, came through the door at the back of the stable. We could hear his printer clacking away. Cy is six feet four with a thick mop of curly hair and glasses. He always looks as if he's got a terrible problem. He said hi to me in his absentminded way.

45

"This is Lilac Kingsmith," I said. "She's staying with us."

Cy is not into the real world. He looked down at this scrubby little kid and said, "Do you know anything about computers?"

She scowled up at him and said nothing.

"I don't suppose you do," he said. "Man, have I got a problem!" He strode on out of the stable on his stork legs.

"Is he crazy?" Lilac said.

Maddie laughed. "He's kind of a genius, and maybe they're a little crazy. You want to ride around the paddock on one of the horses, Lilac?"

Lilac backed away as if Maddie had threatened her.

"Hey, you don't have to," Maddie said.

But Lilac was already outside, heading toward home.

"I better go," I said. "She'll get lost."

"An odd one, huh?"

"Kind of. Talk to you later." I had to run to catch up with Lilac.

Of course we had to wait awhile longer for Diantha to finish her eyelashes. She came out looking like Miss Well-Groomed, clutching Mom's American Express card and MasterCard. "Here, take these before I lose them." She gave them to me, and I put them in my jeans pocket. We got into the second-hand Subaru that Diantha got for her birthday, and she headed downtown to our one decent department store.

She stopped in front, not in the parking lot. "Listen," she said, "Mom said for me to go with you,

46

but you don't need me. I promised this guy I'd meet him for coffee. I'll pick you up in front in about an hour."

She wouldn't have been any help anyway, I knew. She'd have been off in the misses department, looking at things for herself.

"I'm going to get me a swimsuit," I told Lilac. She was staring around the store as if she'd never seen one before. Maybe she hadn't. "I'll come with you first. You want to look at jeans and T-shirts? Kids' things are on the second floor." I led her to the escalator.

She pulled back. I remembered when I used to be scared of escalators. I thought I'd go right on down the underside and never be seen again. "Come on, it's okay." I took her hand. She resisted, but I kind of jerked her on. "Just hold on to the side. You're all right. When we get to the second floor, just step off."

Her jaw was set. She wasn't liking this.

"Now," I said, and I took a big step off at the second floor. She stumbled and half fell against me. "See?" I said. "Nothing to it. The kids' stuff is over against the wall."

"I can do it myself," she said.

"One of us is supposed to help you."

"I can pick out my own clothes."

I didn't know what to do. Mom would say go with her, but I hated to have anybody standing over me when I shopped. "Well, all right. I'll see you down at the main entrance when you're ready. Or if you don't want to go down the escalator alone, wait for me here." I gave her Mom's MasterCard.

"What's that for?"

"Use it to charge your things." Maybe she had never seen a credit card. "It's like money. Just sign Mom's name."

She wandered off as if she didn't know where she was going, but she sure wasn't going to ask directions. I watched her for a minute, not sure she should be doing her shopping alone. It was kind of like throwing her into deep water and saying "Swim." But she had to learn sometime. I couldn't believe she had never seen a credit card. Maybe I should have told her about how much it was safe to spend without starting a scene at home. Oh, well.

It took me quite a while to find a swimsuit I liked. Then I looked for a terry-cloth robe, preferably short and blue. While I was trying robes on, one of the saleswomen came over and asked me if it was all right for a little girl on the second floor to be using my mother's credit card. The clerk was afraid she had stolen it. Everybody knows me in that store, and I had forgotten they wouldn't know Lilac. I told her it was okay.

When I went to the main entrance, Lilac was waiting. She had several fairly big parcels. "What'd you buy?" I said.

"Oh, just some stuff."

"I got a nifty swimsuit," I said. "Dark blue, tank type. And a beach robe. When we go up to the farm, we'll be only a mile from the shore. They have a good beach. Ours here is rocky, and the surf comes in too big. Do you like to swim?"

"I never did it," she said. "We don't live anywhere near water."

"Not even a lake?"

48

She shook her head. "There's a river, but it's polluted."

Diantha hadn't come, of course, so we went into the ice cream place next door and had hot fudge sundaes. Finally Diantha came, and of course when we came out, she said impatiently, "Where were you? Why can't you ever be on time?"

When we got home, Jay was eating a sandwich. He had changed into shorts and a T-shirt. Lilac looked at him, and then she said, "I'm going to go put on my new clothes."

I made us some grilled cheese sandwiches while she was gone, and Jay talked about the horse he had ridden. We heard Mom running a shower, so I put on the water for her coffee.

A few minutes later, I was at the stove, flipping the sandwiches over on the grill, when I heard Jay gasp. I turned around, and there stood Lilac, in tan twill jodhpurs almost exactly like Jay's, a bright-purple hooded sweatshirt with MAINE in white letters across the chest, and red jogging shoes.

"How do you like it?" she said.

At that moment my mother, still in bathrobe and slippers, came into the kitchen, looked at Lilac, and sank heavily into the nearest chair.

chapter 6

Before my mother could pull herself together, Diantha came in. She looked at Lilac and said, "Why are you wearing Jay's jodhpurs?"

"She isn't," Jay said. "She couldn't be. I just took mine off two minutes ago."

"They're Lilac's," I said. "You told her to buy some new clothes, so she did."

"She'll have to take them back," my mother said. "Diantha, I thought I told you to help them shop."

"Mother," Diantha said, "you have always bragged to your friends that your children picked out their own clothes."

"She's not my child," Mom said. "I need some coffee."

"She's your child for the summer," Diantha said.

I was surprised and pleased at the way Diantha was sticking up for Lilac, although I knew it was partly to get herself off the hook for leaving us alone.

Lilac's mouth had set in a stubborn thin line. "I'm not taking them back."

"I think she looks cool," Jay said.

"Me, too," I said, crossing my fingers. "That's a real pretty shade of purple."

"After all, they'll be at the farm," Diantha said. "Grandma isn't going to care what she wears as long as she's clean."

"Who said I'm not clean?" Lilac demanded fiercely.

"Nobody said it," Diantha said. "Relax. I'm on your side."

"Me, too," Jay said. "Those are great shoes. What kind are they?"

Lilac turned her foot so he could see the logo.

"SAS," Jay said. "Those are good shoes."

Lilac began to relax, but she kept a wary eye on Mom.

Mom had gulped down her coffee and began to look a little less groggy. Mornings are not her best time. "I'll drive you to the farm this afternoon," she said. "Pack what you need." She looked at Lilac. "Did you get anything else? Underwear? Pajamas?"

"Never wear 'em," Lilac said.

"But you *have* to wear—"

I interrupted. "I've got some I've never used. Don't worry about it."

"And what did you buy?" Mom said to me. "Or dare I ask? You need shorts and T-shirts and a pair of jeans—"

"I got a swimsuit and a robe."

Mom groaned and put her head in her hand. "Be ready to leave at two," she said.

Upstairs Diantha said, "I'm not being critical, but why did she buy jodhpurs? There aren't any riding horses at the farm."

51

"She hates horses anyway," I said.

"Then why?"

"I think she thinks Jay is cute."

Diantha looked amazed and then she burst out laughing. In a few minutes I heard her telling Amalie on the phone. "You won't believe it," she was saying. "This funny little kid from up north has a crush on Jay. She bought a pair of jodhpurs just like his."

I shut her bedroom door so Lilac wouldn't hear her. Lilac was in her room. "Packing," she said. What did she have to pack?

We had to start all over on lunch because Jay had eaten the grilled cheese sandwiches. At two o'clock on the dot Lilac came downstairs again, lugging that stupid suitcase. A little piece of a shirt stuck out at one end, the shirt she had been wearing before she bought her new wardrobe. And some time or other she had retrieved the clothesline that had been hanging out the window of the other bedroom.

Mom was looking cheerful, I suppose, at the prospect of getting us off her hands. She whistles between her teeth when she's feeling good. It's not the greatest thing to listen to, but we've learned not to make any cracks about it because we don't want to ruin the mood.

Just as we got our bags and ourselves into the wagon, I heard the telephone ringing. "Phone, Mom."

"Oh, let's go quickly. It's probably Jan Hansen wanting me to be on her table at the church fair." She started the engine.

"Aren't you going to work at the fair?" Our

church always has a humongous fair that lasts all day and has dancing at night.

"Yes, but not on Myrna's table."

As the car began to back down the drive, Diantha yelled from an upstairs window. "Hold on! Phone!"

"Tell her I'll call her back," Mom shouted.

"It's Dad."

"Oh, shoot. What's up now?" She shut off the engine. "I'll be right back. I hope he doesn't want to bring somebody home for dinner." She went into the house.

"Why do you have people to dinner?" Lilac said. "And why doesn't she want to?"

"My father brings home a client sometimes. PR and all that. And Mom hates to cook."

We waited for what seemed a long time. I tried to think of something to say to fill the silence, but I couldn't think of anything.

Finally the back door slammed, and Mom came out looking grim. "Out," she said.

"Out?" I didn't know what she meant.

"O-u-t. Take your things. I have to go to the hospital."

That scared me. "Has something happened to Dad?"

"Your grandfather had a heart attack."

"Granddad!" I grabbed her arm. "Will he die?"

"Of course not." She didn't sound convincing. "They're talking bypass. Your father is there. I have to go, Ellis. Get out of the car."

We got out. "Where's Grandma?"

"At the hospital, naturally." She slid the car

into gear and backed out of the driveway too fast.

We went inside. Jay was in the kitchen, and Diantha was just coming down the stairs. They looked upset.

"He won't die, will he?" Jay said. He adores our grandfather. We all do, but especially Jay. When he was little, Grandma used to call him "Jack's little shadow."

"My aunt Min had a heart attack," Lilac said. "Died right there in the kitchen."

"Shut up, Lilac!" Diantha said. I had never heard her say *shut up* before.

Indignantly, Lilac said, "I'm just telling you—"

"Well, don't," Diantha said. "Take her upstairs or somewhere, Ellis."

But Lilac was already slamming out the back door. I let her go. "Did you listen in?" I said to Diantha.

Usually she denies it, but this time she nodded. "Dad sounds very worried."

"Well, I guess that solves who's going when to the farm," I said.

Jay started for the door. He looked very pale.

"Where are you going?" I said.

"I'm going to ride my bike to the hospital."

"They won't let you in," Diantha said. "Children aren't allowed."

"I'll sneak in."

"Jay, those hospital corridors are crawling with nurses, doctors, aides, everybody. You wouldn't even make it to the elevator," Diantha said.

"How do you know?"

"I went to see Terry when she had mono. You can go in if you're over sixteen."

54

He didn't want to give up. "Will somebody call us so we'll know?"

"Jay . . ." Diantha spoke more gently than usual. "Granddad will make it. People have bypasses every day. He'll feel a lot better later. He won't have those angina pains."

"Lilac said—"

"Oh, Lilac." A sudden thought struck Diantha and me at the same time. "If she can't go out to the farm, we'll be stuck with her all summer."

"Not me," I said, "not in August."

"Not me," Jay said. "I have a job."

"Well, certainly not me," Diantha said.

"And Mom has the thrift shop."

"She can't stay here alone," Diantha said. "She'll have to go back."

"Oh, for crying out loud," Jay said, "lock her in Chester's old run, why don't you." Chester was a dog we had once that ran away. "I'm going out to the shed. Call me if you hear anything." He yanked open the screen door and nearly fell over Lilac, sitting on the steps. "Eavesdroppers never hear anything but shit about themselves," he said fiercely, and disappeared in the direction of the barn.

"Jay's learning bad language," Diantha said. "Pretty soon he'll be saying—"

I interrupted her. "Never *mind* that. He's very upset."

"Who isn't?" Diantha stormed upstairs, and pretty soon I heard her talking to Amalie on the phone. The hospital couldn't get us even if they tried. I went upstairs and said, "Get off the phone."

She kicked me in the shin and slammed her bedroom door behind me.

55

I went into my room, slammed *my* door, and said all the prayers I could think of including some of the Hail Marys that Maddie had taught me. Out loud I said, "God, I don't know if you're an Episcopalian or a Catholic or a Buddhist or what, but I'm asking you in all those languages, take care of my gramps." And then I finally began to cry.

I guess I fell asleep, because when I opened my eyes, Lilac was sitting on the foot of my bed watching me. I felt like a protozoan under the microscope in the lab. "Well?" I said.

"What happens to me now?" she said.

I know I sounded mean, but I couldn't help it. "You know, Lilac," I said, "I haven't given it a whole lot of thought."

She didn't seem to resent it. "I suppose your mother will kick me out."

"My family are not barbarians," I said. "But I'll tell you one thing: I'm going to give you a haircut."

"Why?" She looked a little surprised. I guess that wasn't what she expected.

"So you won't look so much like Chester." I got up and went into the bathroom to get the scissors. "Get in this chair and put this towel around your neck and sit still."

"Do you know how to cut hair?" she said.

"In about ten minutes we'll know."

chapter 7

I didn't let her look at herself till I was finished. I had never cut anybody's hair before, and I discovered that to get it anywhere near even, you have to keep cutting off more. By the time I got done, her hair was almost as short as Jay's. At least you could see her face, and she didn't look like an abandoned sheep dog.

I turned her around toward the mirror. She stared hard for a long time. "Well, how do you like it?" I said. I snipped the scissors at a loose end I'd missed.

"I like it," she said.

That was the first time I'd heard her say she liked anything since she came. "Come on in the bathroom and I'll give you a shampoo."

I thought she was going to balk, but she came along. She took off her sweatshirt and struggled out of the jodhpurs.

"Wait a sec," I said. "Stay right there." Not that she was likely to go anywhere stark naked. I ran

57

into my room and got into my new swimsuit. Might as well baptize it.

When I came back, she was looking at the bottles in the medicine cabinet. My mother is a prescription freak.

"Come on," I said, "get in the shower." We have a stall shower, so I grabbed Diantha's shampoo and got in with her. I don't think she had tried the shower before, because she jumped a foot when the water came on. We have one of those needle showerheads that you can adjust. I put it on full strength, dumped a handful of shampoo on top of her head, and began to scrub.

She struggled to get away from me. I think she thought I was trying to drown her. So I held her around the waist with one hand while I shampooed with the other. I must have used half a bottle of Diantha's Caswell-Massey Special Shampoo for Lustrous Hair. She sends away for it. It wasn't easy holding Lilac still. She was so skinny, I could feel her bones, and she wriggled around like a demented eel. (I know, eels don't have bones.)

I shampooed her twice, then gave her a good rinsing and washed her neck while I was about it. My swimsuit felt great, nice and flexible. I like a suit I can really swim in, not one of those kooky things like Diantha's.

When I finally turned off the faucet, I had water in my eyes, so for a minute I could hardly see Lilac. She slid out of the shower stall and stood outside shivering. It was clear that she was mad.

"You almost drowned me," she said.

I threw her a clean bath towel, one of the big

58

ones that we take to the beach. She wrapped it around herself and just stood there.

"People don't drown in showers," I said. "At least not usually. I was just trying to give you a good shampoo. That stuff costs ten dollars a bottle." I didn't know whether it did or not, but I knew it was expensive.

I gave her a small towel to dry her hair. I would have given her the hair dryer, but I was afraid she'd electrocute herself. I got a towel for myself and hung my swimsuit in the shower to drip-dry.

She was still in the bathroom when I left. I dressed fast and went downstairs to see if any word had come from the hospital. Diantha said no. She was sitting in the kitchen drinking a cup of tea and drumming her fingers on the table.

"Who will feed the chickens?" she said.

"What chickens?"

"Grandpa's, of course." She sounded snappish.

I began to worry a lot harder about Gramps. When Diantha forgets about herself long enough to think of chickens, it's serious.

"I think I'll drive out there and see if everything's all right."

"Can you milk the cow?"

"Of course I can. I've done it a million times."

"Do you want me to come with you?"

"No. Look after Jay. He's gone off brooding somewhere." She went upstairs and changed into old jeans. It was the fastest I'd ever known her to change her clothes. She took off in her car.

I started to look for Jay; I was pretty sure he'd be in the barn somewhere. But then I decided maybe he wanted to be alone. Also what if the phone rang? So instead I called the hospital to see if I could find out anything.

I really expected I'd never get past the operator. She'd say, "He's resting comfortably." But when I asked for Mr. Jack Worthington's room, she said, "Hold on. I'm ringing them."

My father answered. I was so surprised, I couldn't think for a second. "How is he?" I managed to say.

"Oh, Ellis, hi. He's resting comfortably."

"But how is he really?"

"They're going to do a bypass in the morning. He's sedated, he's not in pain, vital signs looking good. Don't worry, honey."

I told him Diantha had gone out to feed the chickens and milk the cow. For a second he didn't answer, and when he did, he sounded as if he was almost crying. "That was thoughtful of her. I'll go out later. Mother wants to spend the night with Dad."

"Is Grandma okay?"

"She sure is. You know your grandma: 'Her strength is as the strength of ten.' "

I knew from that little joke that Grandma was probably right there. "Give her my love. I'll take care of Jay and all."

"Your mother says call the pizza place and get them to send you out some food. I better hang up now, sweetie. Don't worry."

I felt better for having talked to him. So then I did go to look for Jay and found him sitting in the barn with his arms wrapped around his knees, staring into space. I told him what Dad had said.

He looked at me. He'd been crying. "Is that good or bad?"

"It sounded good." I told him about Diantha and about the pizza.

"Let's call them now," he said. "I want pepperoni and cheese and sausage."

Somehow I had forgotten all about Lilac. When Jay and I went into the house, there she was in the kitchen eating a cold unbuttered bagel. She was in her jodhpurs and sweatshirt and her short hair looked almost dry, and surprisingly curly.

Jay stared at her. "What happened to her head?" he said.

"I gave her a haircut and a shampoo."

"It's not as short as yours," Lilac said to him as if she would punch him if he said he didn't like it.

"Looks good," he said. "What do you want on your pizza?"

"Did your grandfather die yet?" she said.

Jay winced.

I was furious. "He's not going to die, and if you don't quit saying things like that, you can lock yourself in your room and forget about the pizza." I sounded like my mother.

"I was just showing interest," she said sulkily.

"Well, don't."

The pizza parlor number was stuck to the refrigerator door with a magnet from the dentist that said WE CATER TO COWARDS.

"What do you want on your pizza?" I said to Lilac.

She looked embarrassed, and *that* was something new. I didn't think anything could faze her. And why a simple question like that? "Make up your mind."

"Same as what you get," she said.

It dawned on me that she might never have had a pizza. Maybe way up wherever it was she lived they didn't have them. I called the number and ordered two with pepperoni, cheese, and sausage, and a small one with anchovies for me. I didn't think Lilac was the anchovy type.

"Have we got any money?" Jay said.

I found a twenty-dollar bill and some fives in the cream pitcher where Mom keeps cash.

Diantha came home a couple of hours later, looking tired and dirty. I've seen her look tired after some of her big nights out, but I couldn't remember seeing her in dirty, rumpled jeans.

"That rooster makes me so mad," she said.

"Why?" Jay asked. He and Lilac and I had been watching *Simon and Simon*.

"He won't let the hens eat until he's had all he can stuff into himself. Talk about macho!"

I started to tell her about talking to Dad, but she had called the hospital, too.

"Dad said for you guys to go to bed at ten. They'll be home sometime this evening. Or Mom will. Dad may stay over. The surgery is at eight in the morning. Gramps was asleep when I called."

"Probably doped to the gills," Lilac said. She turned away from the dirty look I gave her, and announced, "I'm going to bed now."

Diantha watched her go out of the room. "She looks like somebody threw a hatchet and she forgot to duck. Who did that coiffure?"

"I did," I said. "And never mind the wisecracks."

"What a summer to get stuck with a kid like that," she said. She yawned and went upstairs.

Jay and I watched TV till ten. I was still awake when Mom came in. I went out to talk to her, but she was too tired and worried to talk. She just kept saying, "Don't worry."

I didn't think I'd sleep a wink, but I did. When I woke up, it was almost nine. It took me a few seconds to remember that Gramps must already have been in surgery almost an hour. I leaped out of bed and banged on Diantha's door. She wasn't there, and that really scared me. She's never up so early.

I found Jay in the kitchen drinking milk. "I've got to call the hospital," I said.

"Hold it. Di called already. They operated at seven instead of eight. He's out, and so far, so good. He's in intensive care. Mom and Di are at the hospital. Dad says everything's looking good."

I sank into a chair, limp with relief. So far, so good; so far, so good. Hang in there, Gramps!

Lilac came in from outdoors.

"In case you're interested," I said, "our grandfather is out of surgery and doing fine."

"I hope there won't be any relapse," Lilac said.

Jay looked at her, and suddenly he laughed. "Lilac," he said, "I hope when I'm stricken with some incurable disease, you'll be there to cheer me on."

chapter 8

Granddad was out of intensive care, but he would have to stay in the hospital awhile. Grandma was back home, but she drove in for visiting hours every day. Dad had found a man to help out with the cow and chickens and whatever else Grandma needed done. Diantha went out there a couple of times and spent the night with her, but Mom didn't think us kids should go yet.

I felt as if I hadn't seen Maddie for years. Her dad had been down to Massachusetts with a horse he had sold, and he told me they were looking forward to my coming. He probably made that up, but it was nice to hear. I just didn't want to think too much about what would happen if they couldn't have Lilac at the farm.

There was a polo game coming up, and Jay was excited about his first time at being an exercise boy.

I took Lilac all around town, to the Dairy Queen, to the mall, to the movies. I bought her some underwear and pajamas, to make my mother happy.

But on a Thursday morning at breakfast, the second Thursday she was there, I said, "I'm going over to see Maddie. You can come if you want."

"No, thank you," she said.

I thought it was because the horses scared her. "You don't have to go near the stable. You can sit on the front porch and shoot the breeze with Maddie's mother. Or you can go in the shed and watch Maddie's brother fool with his computers, if you don't interrupt him." I had watched him myself a couple of times. I don't think he even knew I was there.

"No, thank you," she said.

Mom had gone off to her bridge club. She had told me to keep an eye on Lilac, but I didn't see why Lilac was *my* responsibility. Frankly, I was sick of her. Nothing I did seemed to please her. "I'll be back around four," I said. I thought it might be wise to get home before Mom came and found Lilac prowling around the house by herself.

Lilac shrugged in her usual way. "Whenever," she said.

Diantha came downstairs dressed for sailing. She had specific costumes for specific activities. "Hi, you guys," she said gaily. "If Mom asks, I'm going sailing with some of the kids."

"Whose boat?"

"Oh, you don't know him. You kids got something to do to amuse yourselves?"

When Diantha had gone, I said to Lilac, "What will you do here by yourself?"

She smiled her small secret smile. "I'll think of something."

That was what I was afraid of. But I had my

65

own life to live, didn't I? "See you later, then." I rode my bike over to Maddie's feeling guilty, but also glad to be free.

Maddie had just come back from riding. She was flopped in a lawn chair under the maple tree in the middle of their so-called lawn. I sat in the other canvas chair. "Little Ellis, free at last."

She giggled. "Are you going to be stuck with that kid all summer? What about the Equestrian Center?"

"We can always send her back home."

"Oh, the poor kid. You should have brought her."

"I asked her. She said no. She's scared of horses. Listen, don't make me feel any guiltier than I already do."

"What grade is she in?"

"She's in the fifth grade, and she's ten years old."

"Well, it's too bad she doesn't like horses. Anytime she wants to come over, bring her."

Then we forgot about Lilac and got caught up on all the other stuff that we'd been saving up to tell each other, like about Gramps's operation and her mother's visit to some Italian relatives in Portland, and which of our friends were doing what. It was after four before I knew it.

I rode home fast to get there before Mom did. I didn't see Lilac, but I guessed she was in her room or maybe sitting up in what used to be the hayloft in our barn-garage. For some reason, she liked it up there, maybe because it was dark and cool and still smelled of hay.

I got some pork chops out of the fridge and

66

stuffed them the way Mom does, and got them ready to bake. I set the table, and made some cole slaw. When I'm feeling guilty, I turn into a model child for a short time.

Jay came home, looking filthy. He'd been helping his friend build a boat. When he came downstairs a little later, showered and clean, he said, "Where's Lilac?"

"I guess she's in her room."

"No, she isn't. The door's open, and she's not there."

"I don't know. I asked her to go to Maddie's with me, but she wouldn't go. She's probably just wandering around, exploring. She's getting to know her way around town pretty well."

Jay frowned. "She shouldn't go downtown alone. I mean, she doesn't know where not to go, like Water Street, for instance. All those bars and everything. It's a tough district."

I exploded. "Listen, if you're so worried about her, why don't you take her with you once in a while? Why doesn't Diantha? How come I get stuck with her all the time?"

Jay never gets mad back at me, or hardly ever. Calmly, he said, "Saturday's the polo game. Why don't you bring her to that? She doesn't have to get anywhere near the horses. Then the next day I'll take her someplace after I finish at Mr. Ryan's."

"All right," I said. "Thanks. I'm sorry I yelled."

"Next week I'll take her down to the shore. She said she's never seen the ocean."

"How can you grow up in Maine and never see the ocean?"

"Easy, if you live inland. What's for dinner?"

He took a banana from the fruit basket.

I got him to wash some celery, and I went up to take a shower. It had been good to see old Mad and the horses, and to be on my own for a little while.

When I came downstairs, both Mom and Dad had come home. Mom was pleased with me for fixing the dinner. "Where's Lilac?" she said.

Before I had a chance to answer, Dad came into the kitchen for his Diet Coke. "Where's the little girl?" he said.

"She wanted to be by herself for a while," I said. Mom was giving me a hard look, so I ended up telling the truth. "I wanted to see Maddie, but Lilac didn't want to go."

Dad frowned. "She shouldn't be wandering around alone, should she? She doesn't know the town."

"Well, it won't happen again. Jay and I have worked out a system. I'll go see if she's in the barn or anyplace."

Of course she wasn't. Time went by. Dad listened to the evening news. Diantha came home, too euphoric to pay attention to family problems. The dinner was ready. We sat down to eat.

"I'll have to have a talk with Lilac," Mom said. "She shouldn't go off without telling anybody where she's going. And she really must be on time for dinner."

"Maybe Lilac went back home," Jay said. "Only she doesn't have any money, does she?"

"Who knows?" my mother said. "I don't know how I get into these things."

I went and looked in the pitcher where Mom kept money—the cash cache, Dad called it.

"You don't think she steals, do you?" My mother looked shocked.

"How do I know? How much was in here?"

"About fifteen dollars as of this morning."

"Well, if she's a thief, she's pretty small-time. There's fourteen here now."

"I took a dollar," Diantha said. "I was short."

Dad said, "I think I'll just call the bus station and ask Harry if somebody four feet tall got on the Bangor bus."

All of us, even Diantha, listened nervously while Dad called Greyhound. "Harry? This is Johnny Worthington. Do you happen to know if a little kid by herself got on the Bangor bus this afternoon?"

I was holding my breath, even though I didn't think she would go back home of her own accord.

"Right," Dad said. "We've got this youngster staying with us for the summer, and she seems to have disappeared. . . . Thanks, I'd appreciate it." He hung up. "He'll let us know if she shows up." He looked out the window. "I think I'll just cruise around downtown, just in case."

"She couldn't just *disappear*," Mom said. "This isn't New York City, for goodness' sake."

"People can disappear anywhere," Diantha said. "All it takes is—"

"Never mind," Dad said. "Let's don't indulge in wild speculation."

"She must be really roasting in that sweatshirt," I said. It was still about eighty-five degrees out, and the breeze we usually get from the ocean hadn't started up.

"That reminds me," Mom said. "While she's gone, why don't you go get the clothes she came in, and I'll just run them through the washer."

I went upstairs to Lilac's room. It looked almost as if nobody had been using it. Nothing was moved. The shorts and shirt were wadded up on the closet floor, but nothing was hung up. I looked in the bureau drawers. They were empty except for the pajamas and underwear I'd bought her, still in their plastic wrappings. At first I couldn't see her suitcase. Then I found it under the bed. She must not have unpacked whatever was in it. I knelt beside it and wondered just how sneaky it would be to take a look inside. Curiosity beat out my sense of honor. I began to untie the clothesline, but she had tied it in a very tight knot. It was just beginning to loosen when I heard someone coming up the stairs.

I backed off and got to my feet fast. I didn't want anybody, even Jay, to see me looking in somebody's private suitcase. But it was Diantha, and she just called in to me as she went by: "Mom says hurry up with those dirty clothes, and bring the towels from the bathroom so she won't waste a whole wash on just Lilac's things."

I picked up the shorts and shirts, got the towels, and went downstairs.

"Do you think we should call the police?" my mother said. She put the things in the washing machine and started it up.

"They won't do anything about missing persons for twenty-four hours," Jay said.

"How do you know that?" I said.

"I just know."

I went outside again and searched every inch of the barn again. I asked Mrs. Maguire next door if she had seen a little girl in jodhpurs. That was a

70

mistake. Mrs. Maguire has a mind like the *National Enquirer.*

"Has that little orphan disappeared?" she said. "Oh, my heavens! You can't even go out in broad daylight these days without somebody attacking you. You've seen those pictures of missing kids on the milk cartons, haven't you? Child porn, that's what happens to them. In my day we called it white slavery."

I tried to tell her that a) Lilac was not an orphan, and b) we thought she might just have gotten lost; but she was already rushing in to tell Mr. Maguire that the Worthingtons' little orphan had been snatched.

I was really getting mad at Lilac for causing all this trouble and worry. A ten-year-old ought to have *some* sense. She wasn't used to towns. Ours isn't all that big, but it was a metropolis compared to where she came from. She should have known enough not to go downtown by herself. If that was where she went.

The phone was ringing when I came into the house. My heart began to thump, but it was only Maddie. I started to tell her about Lilac, and she said, "Oh, I saw her in Sanford's, looking at TVs."

Sanford's was the store where we'd done our shopping.

"I offered her a ride home," Maddie said, "but she said she had things to do. She's kind of a weird kid, isn't she?"

"Yes," I said. "Listen, I'll call you back. Everybody's looking for her."

My father came in just then, saying he hadn't seen her.

71

"She's okay," I said. "Maddie saw her in Sanford's."

My mother fell into the nearest chair and exhaled. "I could spank her," she said, "worrying us like that. That young lady and I are going to have a talk. Rules. We need rules."

"Should I go get her?" Dad said.

"No," Mom said. "She got there under her own steam, she can get home the same way. And I'm going to ground her for one week."

"Good," I said. That meant I could come and go without hauling Lilac along.

"I ought to ground you, too," Mom said, "for leaving her alone. Oh, why do people dump these responsibilities on me?"

"You could send her home," Dad said. "You're not committed to keeping her, are you?"

"Well, I promised Frances Hallowell—"

"Frances Hallowell," Dad said, "is not the czar of this town."

"Czarina," Jay said, but nobody paid any attention to him.

I was the one who first saw Lilac coming into the yard. It was just starting to get dark. "Get out the instruments of torture," I said. "Here she comes."

"All right," my mother said. "As soon as she comes in, leave me alone with her."

"Better hear her story first," Dad said. "The accused is entitled to a plea for mercy." He went into the living room and settled down to watch the ball game.

Lilac came into the kitchen, beaming, and carrying an armload of packages all done up in Sanford's wrapping paper.

72

"Lilac," my mother said, "do you realize what time it is?"

"I know I missed dinner," Lilac said, "but that's all right. I hadn't finished my shopping." She put the packages on the kitchen table. "I brought you some presents because you're all so nice to me."

I had never seen her look so pleased with herself. But presents? She didn't have any money that I knew of. Not even an expert could have ripped off Sanford's with that much stuff. And if it was wrapped . . . Suddenly I remembered something. Mom's American Express card was still in my jeans pocket upstairs, and the MasterCard was still in Lilac's possession. And I had told the salesladies at Sanford's that it was okay to let Lilac use it!

"For you, Mrs. Worthington," she was saying as she handed my mother what turned out to be a two-pound box of Sanford's special chocolate creams. I happened to know they were six bucks a pound.

My mother was taken aback, and my mother is not often shook. "Why, Lilac," she said, "you shouldn't have." But she was already opening it. My mother is a chocolate freak.

"And for Mr. Worthington." She handed a flat package to Dad, who had come out to greet the prodigal. It was one of those neckties that look like a fish.

My father swallowed and said, "Well, well. Look at that. Thank you, Lilac, but you shouldn't have done it."

She gave me a bright green straw hat. "It suits you," she said. "As soon as I saw it, I said to myself, that's Ellis."

"Really?" I looked at it. It would have looked

73

good on one of those horses that used to wear straw hats with cutouts for their ears. Maybe Tempest would like it, I thought. I was beginning to feel hysterical.

Diantha got a Linda Ronstadt tape. The last package was for Jay. "Guess," Lilac said to him.

Jay looked embarrassed. "I dunno."

"Open it."

He opened it slowly, wishing he didn't have to. It was a ring, gold, or, anyway, gold-looking, with a big square red stone like a ruby. Jay looked as if he wanted to fade into the wallpaper. "Thanks," he said. "But I don't wear . . . uh . . . jewels."

"Try it on." She took it and started trying it on his fingers. It was a perfect fit for his thumb.

"Lilac," my father said, "did you win the sweepstakes or something?"

"Not exactly." She gave him an angelic smile. "See, I was walking along this street, and a real old lady was trying to mow her grass. It was about three feet high. I felt sorry for her, so I told her I'd do it. She gave me a glass of iced tea and quite a lot of money." She beamed at all of us. "It was hard work."

"What old lady?" I said. "What street?" It was the phoniest story I ever heard.

"Oh, I don't know my way around very well. I don't know the name of the street. She said she really appreciated it."

"I'll bet," Diantha said. "I'll bet she did, Lilac." She raised her eyebrows and went upstairs to play her tape.

My father looked at Lilac a minute and then said, "I've got to see how that game comes out." He left.

My mother was looking puzzled and uncertain. I could see her thinking, We have this child here so we can help her build her character. I can't accuse her of lying when she's tried so hard to be generous. What she actually said was, "Well, Lilac, you were very thoughtful, but I really don't want you going off by yourself like that. It's not safe. We were very worried."

Lilac hung her head. "I'm sorry I worried you. I just didn't know how late it was." She held up her arm. "That's why I thought I'd better get myself a watch. They were on sale."

I had this awful feeling it was going to be a Rolex, but it was a Timex.

My mother stood there as if she thought she ought to say more, quite a lot more, but in the end she gave up. "Get to bed early, all of you." She went to join Dad, although she hates baseball.

Lilac said, "I think I'll go lie down. It's kind of a long walk."

"You should have bought a Buick," Jay said, "to save yourself all those steps."

She looked at him blankly and went upstairs.

"What happened to the grounding?" Jay said to me. "What happened to the instruments of torture?"

I told him about the MasterCard.

He groaned. "When Dad gets the bill, I hope I'm someplace far away."

"You know who's going to get blamed for it," I said. "Me. Mom will say I should have remembered to get the card back. She'll say Lilac doesn't understand about credit cards; she's just an innocent babe from the woods."

"Do you think there's any way we can get rid

75

of her?" Jay looked at the gaudy ring still stuck on his thumb. "Yuck!"

"You better be careful," I said. "She may consider that an engagement ring."

Jay howled, pulled off the ring, and put it in the pitcher with Mom's money. "Why does everything happen to us?"

There was nothing to do next but approach Lilac herself. She was lying on her bed looking at her watch.

"Lilac," I said, "I forgot to ask you for Mom's MasterCard. Can I have it please?"

"Her what?" Her one green eye and one brown eye looked up at me innocently.

"That card I gave you when you bought what you're wearing." I wanted to say "And everything else," but I didn't feel up to it.

"Oh," she said. "I forgot all about that." She rummaged in her jodhpur pockets and brought it out, then handed it to me. "I don't know much about that kind of stuff," she said.

"You're learning fast," I said. Tomorrow I would return the ring and the straw hat. At least that much would be deducted from the bill.

I dialed Maddie's number. "She came home," I said.

"Is she all right?"

"*She* is. I'm not sure about the rest of us. What we've got here is the youngest con artist in the State of Maine."

chapter 9

I worried about that stupid charge card. Even if I took back some of the things, Dad would get a bill for Diantha's tape and that crazy fish tie, and for Mom's chocolates, which were probably half gone by now. First, I thought, I had to talk to Lilac myself. I rehearsed what I would say. "Lilac, credit cards are just charge cards. At the end of the month the bill comes in, and Dad will have to pay for all that stuff you bought." But I was pretty sure she knew that. In this day and age nobody doesn't know what a credit card is. Maybe she figured she'd be gone by the time the bill came. Maybe that was why she didn't unpack her suitcase.

After breakfast I remembered the clothes that Mom had washed. I made a point of taking them to her room when she was there. She looked surprised.

"Who washed those?" she said.

"We've got a washer and dryer."

"Wow! You guys must be loaded."

I started to say that everybody had a washer and dryer, and then I realized not everybody does. I felt apologetic about our having one. "With three kids," I said, "and Dad and his clean shirt every day, Mom would spend all her time . . ." I didn't finish because I remembered Mrs. Kingsmith had a slew of kids. How did Mrs. Kingsmith wash all those clothes? I thought of a TV documentary I'd seen of India, with a bunch of women washing and scrubbing their clothes in the river.

"Do you want me to help you unpack your suitcase?" I said.

"No!" She stuck out her jaw as if I'd threatened her.

"Your clothes or whatever you've got in there will get all wrinkled."

She laughed. It was the first time I'd heard her really laugh. "What's in there won't wrinkle."

"Well, all right. Do you want to ride our bikes to the beach? It's not much of a beach, but I want to try out my swimsuit."

"I don't have a bike."

"Jay said we could use his."

"You can ride, I'll walk."

So she didn't know how to ride a bike. "Well, we can both walk. It's only about a mile and a half."

So we walked. I lent her a swimsuit I'd outgrown, and we wore our shorts and T-shirts over them because we had to walk through town, and my mother won't let us do that in swimsuits.

All the way there, I was wondering what to say about the MasterCard. I ended up not saying anything. Sometimes I am really chicken.

She couldn't believe the ocean. The tide was out, so we could sit on the sand in the sun. It was a hot day, but the breeze off the water was cool. I wondered if she knew how to swim. Probably not. It didn't make much difference, because the water was so cold, she only waded in up to her ankles and backed right out again. I didn't stay in long myself. Swimming in Maine is not exactly like sitting in a hot tub.

Some kids I knew were there, but as soon as she saw them coming over to talk to me, she took off down the beach and walked around some of the big rocks that are on the edge of the water line. She didn't come back till they were gone.

"If you're ever here by yourself," I said, "keep an eye on the tide. At high tide the water comes in fast around those rocks, and you could get trapped."

I thought she looked scared for a second. But then she said, "Who taught you to swim?"

I could hardly remember, I was so little when I learned. "I guess it was Grandma. Yeah, it was. She started us all off with an inner tube."

"Inner tube?"

"To hold on to till we learned to kick, and then she taught us to stroke. There's a better beach than this about a mile from the farm."

"You look like a fish when you're swimming."

"Like my father's necktie," I said.

She grinned.

"Listen, Lilac," I said, taking a deep breath, "there's something I wanted to tell you about—"

She didn't let me finish. "Can we go home now? I'm freezing." She grabbed her clothes and began putting them on, making such a production of it that I gave up.

When we got home, she disappeared into her room.

I was hoping Dad would get home before Mom did, so I could talk to him. I had decided I had to tell him about the charge card. If I told Mom, she'd throw a fit and blame me for not remembering to ask Lilac to give me back the card. Dad doesn't throw fits.

I was peeling potatoes and thinking about potato farms when he came in, taking off his seersucker jacket.

"It's hot, old girl," he said.

"I know. We went to the beach." I got him his Diet Coke. "Chicken salad for dinner," I said. "And iced coffee."

"Sounds good." He started for the stairs to take a shower.

"Can I talk to you one minute?" I said. "Before everybody gets home?"

"You bet." He led the way into the little room he uses to work in. It's a nice room with big leather chairs and lots of books. I curled up in one chair, and he sat in the recliner, slipping off his shoes.

"Fire when ready," he said.

"Well, you know those presents that Lilac bought us?"

"Yes," he said. "I've given them quite a bit of thought."

"Well, I guess it's my fault, but when Mom sent us shopping the other day, I used the American Express card for my swimsuit and robe, and I gave Lilac the MasterCard to buy her stuff with."

"Not knowing it would be riding pants and a sweatshirt suitable for the Maine woods in midwinter."

"No. I should have stayed with her, I realize that. But the worst thing is I forgot to get the MasterCard back from her."

"Ah." Dad stretched out on the recliner, wiggling his toes in his argyle socks. "The plot thickens. Or a better saying might be the light begins to dawn."

"Yes," I said. "I could take back most of the stuff she bought us, but I suppose Mom's chocolates are almost gone, and Diantha would probably have a fit about giving up her tape. . . ."

"And I," he said, "how would I lift up my head in polite society if I had no necktie that resembled a trout?"

"Exactly."

"Well." He sighed. "We have a problem. Do you think she understands what a credit card is?"

"I could be wrong, but I think she does."

"So we have here a scam."

"Why would she do it?"

"To make us like her? To keep us from sending her home? To get herself a watch she always wanted? She's kind of a sad little kid, isn't she?"

"I guess so. But I wish she'd never come here."

"You don't like her much?"

"She's all right, but she's such a nuisance."

"Well, you're fourteen. Maybe it's time you had to endure a nuisance now and then. I don't mean to sound like Father Seth on one of his less-inspired Sundays, but look at it this way: You kids get pretty much what you want. Lilac probably never has. She doesn't have all the things you take for granted."

I thought about it. "She can't swim and she's terrified of horses. She can't ride a bike."

"She probably never had new clothes of her own, or toys, or maybe much love."

"Oh, I think she's had love. She liked her dad a lot. But he died when she was six. Her mother loves her enough to want her to make something of herself."

"I didn't know that about her father dying. When she was six—that must have been rough."

He scared me, talking that way about her father dying. What if something happened to *him*?

"Wouldn't it be nice if you could bring some joy into that kid's life this summer? Even if it is inconvenient?"

I looked at him. "You're talking about my giving up the Equestrian Center, aren't you?"

"I don't know, Ellis. I don't know how things are going to go at the farm. But if you had to, would it kill you?"

"Yes," I said.

He picked up his shoes and took a long swig from his Diet Coke. "Well, your mother has her MasterCard back. When the bill comes in, I'll pay it, and let's not talk about it, even to your mother. It would upset her. Before the summer is over, I'll make a point of letting Lilac understand about charge cards. And letting her know that I know what she was up to. I don't want to make a scene, but sooner or later I'll have to talk to her."

"Meanwhile she thinks she got away with it."

"She must know the bill will come in. Even at the age of ten, she must have learned that everything costs. Thanks for talking to me about it, Shorty."

He hadn't called me Shorty since I was about

five. He was buttering me up for the big sacrifice.

"When you've walked a mile in the other man's moccasins," he said, and went upstairs. That was one of his favorite maxims.

I went out to the kitchen to cut up boiled chicken and celery and avocados. I felt like cutting up Lilac. I was going to get shafted. I could feel it coming.

chapter **10**

Jay spent the next morning trying to teach Lilac how to ride a bike. He was in a very good mood because in the afternoon he would have his first experience as an exercise boy at a polo game. I could have told him it gets pretty boring, walking up and down leading horses while everybody else is watching the game and eating feasts from their tailgates, but he was as thrilled as if he were going to be part of the game.

I didn't think Lilac would want to get near enough to the horses to watch, and so I would probably miss the game to baby-sit her, but I was wrong. Jay's enthusiasm made her want to go. I don't think she had a clue what a polo game was. As far as I know, we have the only polo club around. Mr. Ryan got it started when he first moved up here. He just sold saddle horses for a while, and then he began to talk up polo. In a couple of years it was so popular, we had two teams of our own. We weren't good enough to challenge the big Massachusetts teams like Hamilton and Dedham, but we were getting better all the time. Mrs. Hallowell had donated a meadow on her estate and had had it plowed and resodded and a small bleachers put in. She had even paid for the uniforms and fixed up the stable that was already there. And that very afternoon her grandson would be riding Tex, I supposed. He was only sixteen, but nobody was about to say no to the Hallowells.

I stayed away while Jay gave Lilac bike lessons. At lunchtime he came in looking discouraged. She was right behind him with adoration in her eyes.

"I forgot how long it takes to learn," he said.

He had learned in about five minutes, but he is very well coordinated. It took me all one day.

My mother came in from the thrift shop as we were finishing lunch. Dad was outside mowing the lawn. "Lilac," she said, "you were so nice to buy us presents, I bought one for you." She put a package on the table.

Lilac looked as if she were torn between pleasure and suspicion. She opened it slowly, then took out a pair of L. L. Bean jeans and a pretty light blue cotton blouse. Her eyes opened wide and she just held them and stared at them.

"I guessed at your size," Mom said. "I hope they fit."

I knew what she was really hoping was to get Lilac out of that heavy sweatshirt and the jodhpurs, which were already grass-stained and dirty.

Without a word Lilac clutched the clothes to her chest and ran upstairs.

"We must teach her to say thank you," Mom

murmured, pouring her first cup of coffee for the day. "What is that for?" She pointed to a picnic hamper that Diantha had been loading up with goodies.

"Believe it or not, Diantha is going to the polo game."

Diantha had usually claimed to be bored by polo, but now there was a fellow playing on one team that she had a crush on. When I observed Diantha's behavior, I longed for some way to skip the rest of my teens. From about fifteen on, they really aren't rational.

But anyway, she and Amalie had offered us a ride to the game, and maybe we'd even get to eat some of the food. There was enough for fifty.

When I went upstairs, I realized that Lilac was taking a shower. She was not much given to showers, especially not in the middle of the day. She must have thought the new clothes deserved it. I peeked in her room to see if she had unpacked her suitcase yet. No, she hadn't. It was still under her bed. I don't know why it bugged me so. I love mysteries, but only when I'm on the inside and know what's going on.

When she finally came downstairs, she really looked good. I think she was disappointed that Mom had already gone back to the shop and Jay had gone to the Ryans'. I told her she looked nice, but it was Mom's and Jay's approval she really wanted. I wasn't very important to Lilac.

I left her to finish her lunch, and went to call Grandma, hoping to catch her before she went to the hospital. She was home.

"How is he?" I said.

"Oh, he really seemed a lot better last night.

86

They've got him starting a few exercises on one of those machines. We're going to get him one to have when he comes home." She sounded tired, but there was a new optimistic note in her voice. She'd really been through a lot, and she's not too strong herself.

"Would it help if I came out and spent the day, maybe tomorrow? I could vacuum and stuff like that."

"Oh, Ellis, it *would* help. Diantha cleaned house for me the other day, but the dirt piles up so fast. I'd love to have you come."

"I'll probably have to bring Lilac with me. I don't want to leave her here alone."

"Of course bring her. I'm eager to meet her. I feel bad that things didn't work out so we could keep her."

I wanted to say she didn't know how lucky she was, but I didn't. My grandmother has a good sense of humor, but she doesn't like jokes aimed at other people.

I decided not to tell Lilac till later that we were going out to the farm. I didn't want to give her time to work up resistance. I knew Dad would drive us; he'd probably be going out there himself. Mom would be expecting me to go to church, but going to help Grandma would be what she'd consider a good Christian alternative.

Diantha and I put the picnic hamper in the station wagon. Di had swapped cars with Mom so we'd have a tailgate for the picnic. When my father asked why people couldn't have a picnic at a polo game without a tailgate, Di said, "But, Dad, everybody has one. That's what it's all about." He gave up.

I was making a big effort to be nice to Lilac, after my talk with Dad. "Doesn't she look nice in her new outfit," I said to Diantha.

"Super," Diantha said, and smiled at Lilac. It was always easier for Diantha to seem nice when she wanted to than it was for me. I guess that's what you call charm.

Lilac actually blushed. "Look at all the pockets." She showed us. "It says L. L. BEAN, see?" She had to twist around to show us the leather label above the hip pocket. "We came by L. L. Bean's on the bus. The driver showed us where it was."

"They're very reliable," Diantha said. She sounded like Mom.

We had to wait while she went to pick up Amalie, and I wondered if I should use the time to explain to Lilac what a polo game was all about. It's no fun to watch a game when you don't know what they're doing. But I couldn't explain it without saying quite a bit about horses, and I was afraid that might put her off going. If she didn't go, I couldn't go. There was no more leaving her home alone.

We sat on the front steps, waiting for Diantha. "They're giving swimming lessons at the Y this summer," I said. "Would you like to go?"

"No," Lilac said promptly.

I tried to think of something to talk about. "Do you go fishing up where you live?"

"Some people do. Not me."

"Where do they fish?"

"If you want to walk about ten miles, there's a lake."

"Do you like to read?"

88

She shot such a suspicious look at me, I thought she must not have heard me right.

"Like books and stuff," I said. "I go to the library a lot. They've got some super books for kids."

"I like animal books," she said.

Hurray. I'd gotten a real answer out of her.

"Me, too. Have you read—" I almost said *My Friend Flicka* till I remembered how she felt about horses. *"The Wind in the Willows?"*

She shook her head. I wondered if that was too young for a ten-year-old. "I've got it in my bookcase," I said. "You can borrow it."

"I like bears," she said, "but you can't get close to them. They'll claw you to death."

"Do they have bears up where you live?"

She looked at me as if I were stupid. "Of course."

"I've never seen a live bear."

She widened her mismatched eyes in astonishment. "That's weird."

I felt underprivileged. "We don't have any here," I said lamely.

"Do you have deer?"

"Well, not here, but I saw one when we went for a drive once."

"We've got deer all over the place, and moose. What animals *do* you have?"

I tried to think of something besides dogs, cats, and horses. "Raccoons? Squirrels."

She dismissed such small fry with a wave of her hand. "This is a weird place."

I was trying hard not to get defensive. I like our town. It's bigger than a village and smaller than a city, and I happen to think it's a neat place. "I'm sorry you don't like it here," I said, sounding huffy in spite of myself.

She gave me that quick, amused grin that meant she knew she'd scored. "New York is where I'm headed for."

"You mean when you're grown up?"

"I mean soon." She gazed off into the distance, mysteriously.

I felt alarmed. What if she really tried to run away to New York? I mean, she's ten years old! "It's not a safe place," I said.

She shrugged. "I can take care of myself."

"What would you do for money?"

She just smiled.

At that interesting moment Diantha pulled up in front of the house and beeped her horn impatiently. We got in the middle seat. Amalie turned around with her too-sweet smile and said, "Hi, Ellis. Hi—you must be Lilac."

Lilac stared down at her feet and said nothing.

"I've heard a lot about you, Lilac. Are you having a good time here? I know the Worthingtons are thrilled to have you."

It was news to me. Lilac said nothing, so I said, "Lilac is kind of shy."

"Oh, I know how that is," Amalie burbled. "When I was your age, I'd just about die if anybody even looked at me."

I wanted to say "Then why don't you turn around and let her alone." But of course Amalie is Amalie, and she asked several more questions that Lilac didn't answer before she gave up and turned back to Diantha. From then on the conversation was all about this boy who was playing on the team.

"Mrs. Hallowell's grandson is playing," I said, just to get in on the conversation.

"That baby?" Diantha said.

"He's almost as old as you are."

"But I'm not playing polo." Both Diantha and Amalie seemed to think that was a very witty reply. They laugh at things about ten times more than makes sense. It's part of the teen syndrome. Maddie and I laugh a lot, too, but only when it's *funny*.

We were going to meet Maddie at the field. Her mother would be there, too; she always comes when Mr. Ryan plays because she's convinced he's going to get hurt, if not killed, and only she can take care of him. She hates horses even more than Lilac does.

Diantha, who is a very good driver, I must say, pulled into the bumpy dirt road that leads to the field. Several cars were moving slowly in front of us, and a lot were parked next to the field on both sides. The field looked green and nice. It has a two-foot-high fence of thin boards painted white that are scarred and dented where the big wooden balls hit it, and sometimes the mallets or a horse's hoof. The field is on high ground, and off to the east you can see the ocean. Some sailboats with bright-colored sails were far out that day, having a race. There's a footpath leading from the polo field to the cliffs that border the ocean. At low tide there's about six feet of hard-packed sand at the bottom of the cliff, but it isn't a place where anybody goes to swim or sunbathe because the sea comes smashing in on the big rocks that extend out into the water. At high tide there's no beach at all.

North of the polo field, just its gabled roof showing, is the Hallowell mansion. Thirty rooms. My
mother says she doesn't know how Mrs. Hallowell
finds people to take care of the place. In fact, nobody
works for Mrs. H. very long except one couple, a cook
and her gardener husband, who have been there for
years. They get along really well with Mrs. Hallowell
because they don't pay any attention to what she
says.

Diantha backed the wagon into an empty space
close to the field, with the tailgate facing the field.
Some people she and Amalie knew were in a Volvo
wagon next to us. They went over to talk to them
while Lilac and I settled down on the tailgate with
the food in the picnic hamper right behind us. I
snitched a couple of bananas and gave one to Lilac.

Exercise boys were walking horses out by the
stable. I pointed out Jay to Lilac.

"When's he going to do his thing?" she said.

"He's doing it. His job is to walk the horses."

"You mean that's *all*?"

"That's it."

"How could he get so excited about just walking
up and down?"

"Well, if you love horses and—" I gave up. How
could I explain that if you love horses, the smell of
the stable, the coming and going of the riders, the
jokes of the hostlers, the whole business, is thrilling.
She'd think I was crazy.

Instead, I pointed out some of the team members
who were riding out of the stable yard, loping around
the far side of the field in their bright clothes. They
all wore white jodhpurs and shiny boots (that would

get less shiny as the game went on); Team A wore scarlet silk shirts, and Team B had lemon-yellow shirts with black stripes. They all wore white helmets. Some of them were knocking a ball up and down with their mallets. Some were still unloading their horses from the horse trailers.

As more and more people arrived in their summer clothes, the whole area seemed to shine with color. It was a perfect day, bright sun in a cloudless sky, and no wind. Polo weather.

As the riders began to come out onto the field, Diantha and Amalie squeezed in beside us on the tailgate. Maddie came bouncing over the grass in her dad's old army jeep with her mother beside her holding on for dear life. The jeep has no top, and Mrs. Ryan always looks as if she expects to bounce out.

"Mrs. Ryan comes only to the games Mr. Ryan plays in," I said. "She thinks he's going to get killed."

"She has reason," Diantha said. "When they lived in Massachusetts, some rich guy got mad in the middle of a game and hit him over the head with his mallet. He was in the hospital with a skull fracture."

"I don't know if I want to watch this game," Lilac said.

"What are you worrying about? You're not playing."

Amalie said, "You could go hold Mrs. Ryan's hand, Lilac." She thought that was funny. Lilac didn't.

"Mrs. Ryan wrings her hands and mutters in Italian all through the game," Diantha said. "Nobody's sure whether she's praying or swearing."

"I don't think it's very nice to laugh at Mrs. Ryan," I said.

Diantha flushed. "I was only kidding. Actually, I like her." She shoved against me. "You kids take up too much room."

"We were here first," I said.

"Let's sit on the backseat," Diantha said to Amalie.

The referee rode out onto the field, and the teams moved into formation. For a moment the horses and riders were as still as a photograph, and then suddenly violent, fast motion erupted everywhere, like when a quiet stream suddenly turns into rapids.

The whacks of the mallets against the big wooden ball were sharp in the still air. Horses bunched up, shouldered each other off, stopped, and turned so fast you could hardly follow them with your eyes. Sometimes they came close to where we were, then swerved and were at the other end of the field. I was watching the Hallowell boy on Tex. I thought he rode him too hard, too tight, but I had to admit he was a very good horseman. Of course, he'd been riding practically since he was born. Tex looked great. Mr. Ryan really knew how to pick horses.

I glanced over at Mrs. Ryan. She had climbed out of the jeep and was leaning against it, her hands clenched together. She wore a big straw hat that shaded her face. Maddie had disappeared, but at the end of the first chukker she came over and sat with us.

"Is it over?" Lilac asked, sounding hopeful, as the players rode off the field.

"Nope. Not yet. But now we can eat."

Diantha and Amalie, who had been kneeling on the seat, got out, and we all pulled the picnic basket onto the tailgate. A couple of Diantha's boyfriends wandered over. There's nothing like food to attract them. There was a lot of giggling and chitchat, but Maddie and Lilac and I concentrated on the food. Maddie had brought some chicken sandwiches for all of us. She tried to get her mother to come over, but Mrs. Ryan was too nervous to socialize. She climbed into the jeep again, and sat there looking like a statue of Tragedy.

"My mother hates the games," Maddie said. "On account of that old accident of Dad's."

You had to eat fairly fast to get your share of the food, especially with those boys there. All they contributed was a couple of wine coolers, for Diantha and Amalie. I don't think they even knew we were around.

"Jay must get thirsty," Lilac said. "Can we take him a Coke?"

"No, we're not allowed near the stable during a game," I said. "He probably has a Coke anyway. There's a machine in the stable."

"Maybe he doesn't have a quarter," Lilac said.

"Don't worry about Jay. He takes care of himself."

By the time the food had disappeared, the horses were coming back onto the field. Diantha was drooling over how wonderfully her friend was riding. Actually, I don't think she knew him beyond the "hello" stage, but she acted as if they were buddies.

"He's the one on the chestnut," she was saying

to one of the boys. "Harris Grover. He goes to Dartmouth."

"Who doesn't," the boy said. He was still in high school. Sometimes I think I'd like to tape what Diantha and her friends say to each other so I could publish it in a book *Witty Sayings of the Teen World*.

The boys drifted away, and Amalie and Diantha climbed back into the seat. "Maddie, I can't see over your head," Diantha said.

"So move," I said. But Maddie was the one who moved. Maddie is a lot better-natured than I am.

Team B was leading. Mr. Ryan was on Team B, and so was my Tex, so I was rooting for them. Mr. Harris Grover of Dartmouth was on Team A, so my sister squealed in our ears whenever A scored.

This time the play seemed even faster and more piled up than before. The referee's whistle rang out often. The Hallowell kid deliberately crashed Tex into another horse, and was ordered out of the game on a foul. A second-string player replaced him. Typical spoiled Hallowell brat.

Suddenly a swirling confusion of horses seemed to come straight at us. I knew how fast they could stop at the low fence and turn, but Lilac didn't. All she saw was enormous, sweaty horses hurling themselves toward her. She screamed, jumped off the tailgate, and ran down the path that led to the cliffs.

"Oh blast that kid," I said. I jumped off the tailgate. I'd have to go get her and miss the rest of the game.

"Let her go," Amalie said. "She'll come back."

But I wasn't about to do that. She had looked really terrified. Who knew what dumb thing she'd do. I ran along the path, and Maddie came right behind me. We could see Lilac ahead of us, getting near the cliffs and not slowing down a bit. I yelled her name a couple of times, but it's hard to run and yell at the same time.

Where the path came out, the cliff sloped down to the water, and you could get up and down it if you were very careful. It would be easy to lose your grip and fall. The tide was in. I could hear the surf pounding on the rocks.

"Lilac, wait!" I yelled. She didn't slow down.

Maddie has longer legs than I have. She raced past me at a dead run, but there was no way she was going to get to the cliff in time to stop Lilac. Lilac was running blind, like a runaway horse. I could see how the horses might have scared her, but she was a long way from them by now and still she didn't slow down. It looked as if she were going to run right off the top of the cliff.

She slowed down just as she came to the edge. We both called to her. She half turned and went over. For a minute all we could see were her hands clutching at the top of the cliff. Then there was nothing to see at all.

Maddie got there first. She tore off her denim jacket and started down the cliff. I thought they were both going to get killed. It took me forever to get to the cliff. I threw myself on the ground and hung over the edge. Lilac was about halfway down, clinging with hands and feet to narrow ledges. You could tell she was scared to move.

Maddie was just above her, moving slowly and carefully. She was talking quietly to Lilac, but I couldn't hear what she said over the noise of the surf. I saw Lilac look down. A wave smashed in and then ebbed, leaving a line of foam. Another one was coming in right behind it, throwing up a curtain of spray as it hit the rocks in the water. I heard Maddie say, "Don't look down! Lilac, look at me." She was almost down to where Lilac was now. She leaned a little sideways and stretched her long arm down to Lilac. I held my breath. I knew how easily the surface of the ledges could crumble under your hand. If only I had a rope! I took off my belt, but it was awfully short. Maybe better than nothing though. I dug the toes of my boots into the ground as far as I could.

"Take my hand and feel for toeholds and a handhold. Move up when I do. I'll take it real slow . . ." I didn't hear the rest of what Maddie said because another wave smashed in. I saw Lilac look up, her face all squeezed with fear.

"Lilac. Take my hand."

Very slowly Lilac flattened herself against the sloping rock and moved her right hand up to meet Maddie's. Thank God for Maddie's muscles, I thought.

When she had Lilac tight by the hand, her long fingers clenched around Lilac's wrist, Maddie moved up a few inches, feeling for holds and waiting for Lilac to move with her.

I don't think I breathed. One little misstep from either of them, and they'd both plunge onto the rocks below them.

I dangled my belt over the edge of the cliff, wrapping it once around my wrist. It was pitiful how short it was. For once I wished I were fat.

It seemed like hours that they were climbing

that short distance. I didn't know what good the belt would be anyway, since Maddie had to use one hand to pull herself up and the other to pull Lilac. If she let go with her climbing hand, she might lose her balance and fall. I almost pulled it back up but decided to let it hang there in case it might do some good.

I could tell when Maddie saw it. She glanced up at me and her eyes looked as if she were saying "Good." I dug my toes in still deeper. The earth was soft.

When Maddie was almost to the top, she let go of the cliff and grabbed the belt. The weight almost jerked me over the cliff myself. I began pulling slowly, hand over hand on the leather belt. Maddie's arm came over the top of the cliff. I wanted to pull hard on the belt then, to get them to the top fast, but it was too risky. Lilac was still about six feet down the cliff. She could still fall.

I began to wriggle backward, pulling. Maddie's elbow jabbed into the ground to give her leverage. Then she boosted herself over the lip of the cliff and leaned down with both hands pulling Lilac up. Lilac came over the top of the cliff fast, and all of a sudden all three of us fell in a heap on the grass, panting.

When I sat up, Lilac had buried her head in her arms and was silently sobbing. Her new blouse was dirty and torn, and Mr. Bean's jeans were covered with dirt stains.

Maddie took a deep breath and got up. "Stay here. I'll get the jeep and take us home."

Lilac didn't move or look up. Her shoulders shook. I sat watching her, wishing I knew what to say.

chapter **11**

The jeep has only two seats, so I had to hold Lilac in my lap. I thought she'd object, but she was so limp, it was as if she were asleep. She didn't weigh anything, even dead weight like that.

Nobody said anything. Maddie isn't old enough to have a license; you have to be fifteen and with drivers ed to get even a junior license, but she had been driving for almost a year, not downtown or very far, but to the polo field and places like that. She looks older than she is.

She took the back roads to my house. "I've got to get back," she said, "to take Mother home. The game must be about over."

Lilac hadn't moved or looked up.

"Thanks for all you did," I said to Maddie. I nudged Lilac. "We're home. You can get out now." I waited for her to say thank you or *something* to Maddie. After all, Mad had saved her life probably. But Lilac just slid out of the jeep and ran into the house. I looked at Maddie. "I give up," I said.

"Listen, don't be hard on her," Maddie said.

"That was one terrified kid. She must have had bad stuff in her life to get as scared as that."

"You were a hero," I said.

She laughed. "Talk to you later." She drove off.

She really had been a hero. I felt kind of bad that it hadn't been me who saved Lilac. I'm always right there *behind* whoever does the noble thing. I don't move fast enough or think fast enough. Maybe I'm a coward at heart.

Lilac was in her room with the door closed. I knocked, and of course she didn't answer. I said, "Throw your jeans out here, and I'll run them through the mini-wash. They'll be dry before Mom gets home." I figured she was scared of what Mom would say when she saw the torn shirt and the messed-up jeans.

I didn't hear anything, and I was about to go away, but then the door opened a crack and the jeans landed on the floor beside me. I really wanted to say something reassuring, but how can you reassure a closed door? I took the jeans downstairs.

Mom *was* going to be mad about the shirt. If I told her the whole story, she was going to think Lilac was really "disturbed," as adults say when they mean crazy. She might even insist on sending the kid home. Nobody wanted her gone more than I did; if she stayed, she might wipe out my dream of the Equestrian Center. But I just couldn't see packing her off home, like returning unsatisfactory goods.

I counted what was left of my allowance. I'd saved most of it to use at the Center, but decided maybe I wouldn't need that much. Maybe I wouldn't need *any*, but I didn't want to dwell on that. I was thinking I could go to Sanford's and get another shirt like the one Mom had bought. But I didn't want to leave Lilac alone in her current state of mind. I wished Diantha would come, but I knew she wouldn't. Anyway, she was probably furious. I had a vague memory of Lilac knocking over the thermos of lemonade when she jumped off the tailgate.

I was sitting in the kitchen, fussing, when I saw the Subaru come into the yard. It was Dad, thank goodness, not Mom. I went out.

"Hey," he said, "did you leave the game early?"

"Sort of. Dad, will you be here awhile? I have to do an errand, and I don't want to leave Lilac alone."

"What kind of errand?" Why do parents always ask questions like that? A person under eighteen has no privacy whatever.

"Where's Mom?"

"Playing golf with Mona Harrod. Which doesn't answer my question."

There was no way out except to tell him the whole story. I tried to make him understand the way it had been, how terrified Lilac was, how brave Maddie was. I wished I could have said I saved her, I said, but all I could contribute was my belt.

Sometimes he seems to read my mind. He said, "That was good thinking, El, giving Maddie the belt to hang on to and reeling her in. You and Maddie . . . you're a good pair."

I felt a lot better.

"That poor little kid," he said. He was taking out his wallet.

He handed me two twenties. "This is on me. Get the child a shirt. No need to upset your mother."

"Thanks a lot, really, Dad. I won't need this much. I'll bring you the change."

"No," he said, "buy something nice for Maddie and something for yourself. Compliments of the house."

I hugged him and ran for my bike. I wanted to get back before Mom came. Then I remembered to ask Dad again if he'd be there for a while.

"Don't worry. And by the way, your grandfather feels a lot better."

"Oh, good!" I felt guilty that I hadn't asked. "We're going out there tomorrow. We'll clean house for Grandma."

He smiled. "She told me."

At Sanford's I went through the kids' blouse section till I found one like Lilac's. I took a chance on a size ten, although it might be kind of big. She was so skinny and small.

There was quite a lot of money left. I bought myself a giant-size Hershey with almonds, and looked around for something for Maddie, something suitable for a person who had just performed a heroic act. Finally, I got her a neat braided leather riding crop with a silver handle. It took the rest of Dad's money and three dollars and twenty cents of my allowance, but it was worth it. I wanted to go and give it to her right away, but I decided I'd better get the shirt to Lilac before Mom got home.

Actually, she had just come in, but I zipped upstairs with my packages before she saw them. In a minute she came up and said, "What's in the washing machine?"

"Just a pair of jeans in the mini. Did you beat Mrs. Harrod?"

"I did." She looked pleased with herself and she forgot to ask any more questions about the washer.

I went downstairs a few minutes later and threw the jeans into the dryer. When I heard Mom taking a shower, I got the shirt and knocked on Lilac's door. "Let me in, Lilac. I've got something for you."

At first I didn't think she was going to, but then the door opened about six inches. I pushed through and closed it behind me.

She was already back on her bed with the quilt pulled over her when I turned toward her. She had her eyes shut tight. I went over and put the package on the bed. "I got you a shirt just like the one Mom gave you. Nobody will ever know the difference."

Her eyes flew open, and she blinked in surprise. I think that was the last thing she was expecting.

I picked up the torn shirt that she had thrown on the floor. "I'll put this one in the trash can outside, so nobody will see it."

"No," she said. "I want to keep it."

"What for? It's too torn up to mend."

"I want it."

"Okay, it's your shirt." I looked at her a minute, wanting to tell her I was sorry I'd taken her to the game and scared her so; but it's hard to talk to somebody who has turned her back on you and is practically invisible under a quilt. I said, "Dinner will be ready at six-thirty, don't forget. Mom gets upset if we're late."

"I'm not hungry," she muttered into the quilt.

"Oh. Shall I tell Mom you have a headache or something?" She didn't answer, so I said, "Otherwise she'll come charging up here."

"All right."

"I'll bring you a sandwich when I bring your jeans."

"Are they wrecked?" Her voice was so small, it was hard to hear her.

"No, they just got dirty. It's hard to wreck Bean jeans." I waited, but she didn't say anything else, so I left. It seemed as if she might have said thank-you or something, but that wasn't Lilac's way, I guess. Anyway, Dad says you don't do nice things for people in order to be thanked. The trouble is, I'm not a noble person.

I told Mom that Lilac had a headache. I was afraid Diantha would hold forth about Lilac's flight, but she gave me a searching look and didn't say a word.

Jay, who was still in a glow from his professional afternoon, said, "Did you guys leave the game early? I came looking for you right after I got through work."

"Yeah, we left," I said.

Dad didn't bat an eye. He's a good secret-keeper.

Afterward, when Diantha and I were stacking the dishes in the dishwasher, she said, "What was the matter with her?"

"Horses scare her."

"She knocked over the lemonade and stepped in Amalie's pecan pie." But she didn't sound mad.

I don't usually confide in Diantha, but since she was being so nice, I told her the rest of the story.

Her eyes widened. "Climbing around on that cliff . . . they could have been badly hurt."

"You're telling me! I was scared spitless."

"That child needs to see a therapist."

"Don't tell Mom, okay? She gets so shook over things."

"Of course I won't."

105

Later I rode over to Maddie's and gave her the riding crop. She was really pleased. She kept saying it was just what she wanted.

Her dad came in and told me what a good job Jay had done. "That lad's so conscientious, it makes me want to tell him to take it easy." Mr. Ryan is a small, wiry man with smiley blue eyes. He's very kind and nice.

I told him it was the greatest day of Jay's life.

"He'll be playin' out there himself one of these days."

"Breaking his bones," Mrs. Ryan said.

Mr. Ryan laughed and rumpled her hair. You wouldn't think she was a woman who would stand for that, but she just laughed and shook him off.

"You all packed for the Equestrians?" he asked me.

"In my head anyway." Then I said, "Mr. Ryan, if anything should happen that I couldn't go, would it be a problem for them?" My heart sank, just putting the possibility into words.

"No, no. Just let Hank know ahead of time." Unlike my parents, he didn't ask any questions.

When I got home, Lilac's door was still shut. What if this afternoon's trauma had scarred her for life? I went to the kitchen and fixed her a couple of roast beef sandwiches and put them on a tray with a glass of milk. I got her jeans out of the dryer and went upstairs. I put my big Hershey bar on the tray, knocked on the door, and when she didn't answer, I went in and put the tray on the table beside her bed. She was sound asleep. The shirt I had bought was spread over her shoulders, on top of the quilt.

chapter **12**

When I came downstairs the next morning, Lilac was sitting in the kitchen holding an envelope. She was wearing the clean jeans and the new shirt.

"How you feeling?" I said.

"All right." She took a twenty-dollar bill out of the envelope. I noticed there was one at my place, too. Dad had written on the envelope, "July allowance, paid in advance to compensate for summer expenses. Sign here." And there was an inked line for our signatures. He always makes us sign for our allowance. He says we may as well develop proper money habits.

"What is this?" Lilac said. "Why do I have to sign my name?"

Suspicious to the end! I explained about our allowances. I knew Dad had probably given it to us early so Lilac would have some spending money.

"You mean I can just spend it?"

"Or save it or have it for breakfast."

She didn't smile. Lilac was not much for jokes.

She carefully folded the bill into eighths and tucked it into her jeans pocket.

"Don't forget it's there," I said. "I lost a ten-dollar bill to the washer and dryer once."

"Don't worry." She poured herself another glass of milk. Jay's cereal bowl was in the sink with a few dried Rice Krispies stuck to the sides.

"Where's Jay, do you know?"

"He went over to the Ryans'."

"Dad is going to take you and me to the farm. He's getting dressed."

"Do they have horses?"

"No. One cow and some chickens is all. I think Grandma may have sold the cow already. Granddad won't be able to take care of it. Have you been up long?"

"Yeah. I went to early mass."

I was amazed. "You went to church?"

"It's Sunday."

"You didn't go last Sunday."

"I couldn't find the church. Then I saw it the other day."

"What church?"

"St. Mary's."

Catholic. I wondered how Mom would like that. Dad says her bigotry is more social than religious: She grew up in a town where the factory workers were mostly French and Irish and went to the Catholic church, and what he calls "the high mucky-mucks" like Mom's family were mostly Episcopalian or Congregational. Jesus must get discouraged about that kind of thing.

"It was the biggest church I was ever in," Lilac

said. "Maddie and her mother were there. They drove me home."

"Oh. That was nice."

She nodded. "I like Mrs. Ryan."

When Dad came downstairs in his Sunday jeans and sweatshirt, he said, "You ready to go?"

"Aren't you going to eat breakfast?" I said.

"Nope. Your grandmother offered to cook me some buttermilk pancakes."

It was about nine-thirty when we got to the turnoff road toward the coast. The sun was already beating down.

"Going to be a scorcher," Dad said. He always sounded happy when he was going back to the place where he grew up. "I promised to weed the vegetable garden. What I need, El, is that nice straw hat that Lilac gave you."

Lilac looked at him quickly to see if he was laughing at the hat. He wasn't; he's like Grandma that way. "You never wear it," Lilac said to me.

"I guess because I'm not used to wearing a hat, I forget it," I said.

"I'll remind you," she said.

We turned into the long driveway that leads to the house. On one side there was a field of corn, and on the other side just a field where Gramps used to turn out the cows when he had quite a few. Now there wasn't any cow in sight. "Grandma must have sold the cow." I missed seeing old Bess out there. She was a nice cow.

Lilac was noticing everything. I tried to look at the place through her eyes, as if I hadn't seen it before. There was the house, set back in a grove of pines that were weird shapes partly because pitch pines *are* twisted-looking and partly because the salty wind beats on them. Grandma likes them because they make some shelter without shutting out the light. The house itself is big and old—probably a couple of centuries old, Dad figures from records at the courthouse. It's what they called a salt-box type, two stories high with a big attic and a roof that slants in the back, so the kitchen and what used to be a pantry and is now a bathroom are only one story high. It's a nice weatherbeaten gray with a huge central chimney. The kitchen and the living room and two of the bedrooms have fireplaces. There's a wide front door with a brass knocker, and a millstone for a step. Dad will inherit the place when his parents die, but I don't like to think about their ever dying. It wouldn't be the same house without them.

"All ashore that's going ashore." Dad shut off the engine, and we all got out. Lilac was looking and looking. She noticed the big gray barn and the shed where Gramps keeps his tools. She looked at the chickens pecking around outside their hen house. Grandma always has a couple of banties, and this year she had two Favorellis, very pretty buff- and gold-colored with specks of black.

"What pretty hens," Lilac said.

"They've got feathers on their feet," I told her. "They're named Brandy and Peaches. They're Grandma's pets."

Grandma was already coming out to greet us. She's small with a round face; she's prettier than any of her three daughters.

"Will they get eaten?" Lilac asked.

"Not those two. And not the banties. When a chicken is killed, Gramps has to do it. Grandma always grieves, even over the dumbest ones."

Grandma and Dad were hugging each other as if they hadn't seen each other for months. Then she came to us and hugged me. She held out both hands to Lilac. "You're Lilac," she said. "I'm so glad to meet you at last."

Lilac hesitated and then put her hands in Grandma's. I wondered if anybody had ever told Lilac before that she was so glad to meet her at last.

"Come in and have breakfast." Grandma kind of shooed us into the house as if we were her pet chickens. She was wearing khaki pants that were probably Gramps', because they were too big for her. Her faded blue denim shirt hung over the top of the pants, and she was wearing her long gray hair pulled back in a knot.

The house always smelled of the dried herbs and spices that she puts in little bags and hangs in the closet, a mix of clove and cinnamon and other things I forget the names of. The house was cool. In the living room the walls were white, and all the rugs on the wide floorboards had been braided by Grandma and her mother. It was a big room, and the far end, where the light was best, was where she made the quilts that she sold to the summer people. A half-finished quilt hung on the frame, and bright-colored squares of cloth were draped over chairs and on the floor near the machine.

"My house is a mess," she said to Lilac, "but it always is, so I won't apologize. At least I always know where everything is."

Dad laughed. "The scientists have a new theory, Ma, called Chaos. They say what looks like disorder and turbulence really has a pattern. That's how I think of this house."

"Well, I'm glad to know science has explained me. Come on into the kitchen. You all look hungry."

She had set four places at the long trestle table in the kitchen. It's a huge kitchen with the old unused woodstove still in place, next to the electric stove. Gramps's theory is: "You never know when civilization will fail us. We've always got a woodpile."

She and Dad talked about Gramps, how he was feeling, how soon he might come home, and what furniture they should bring downstairs so he could sleep in the den and not have to climb stairs. And while she talked, she was flipping pancakes and pouring coffee and making cocoa. When I was little, I thought it was really true that, as Dad said, she could do six things at once without batting an eye. She always seemed calm, and after you were around her awhile, you felt calm, too.

Lilac's eyes glistened at the big plate of pancakes Grandma set in front of her. There was a small pitcher of melted butter and another of warmed-up maple syrup.

"Dig in, children," she said. She gave Dad his plate and poured herself a cup of coffee. "I miss Bess's cream," she said. "Store-bought isn't the same."

"I suppose you've been up since five," Dad said.

She nodded, then said to Lilac, "I'll bet you get up early, too, Lilac. You're a farm person, like me."

Lilac blinked. She hadn't said a word since we

got there, but she was watching Grandma with an expression on her face that I hadn't seen before. I wasn't sure what it was, but it was not her usual "stay off of my back" look.

"Do you get up at five, too?" Dad asked her.

"In November we get up at four," she said. She was answering him, but she kept her eyes on Grandma.

"Why in November?" Dad said.

"School's closed. We work in the potato fields."

Grandma looked shocked. "They close the school and put the children to work in the fields?"

"Sure. Nobody else will do that work."

"But that's stoop-labor," Grandma said to Dad. "Closing the schools and making the children do stoop-labor. That shouldn't be allowed."

"We get paid," Lilac said. "Not much, but some. It helps out."

"Good heavens," Grandma said. There was silence for a few minutes except for the sounds of people eating, and the radio in the other room playing the Jazz Revisited program. Grandma loves jazz from the thirties and forties. She and Grandpa met at a ballroom in Hampton Beach, and he always says he fell in love with her because she was such a good dancer. She's told us about that place lots of times. It was very big, and it had colored chandeliers that revolved and threw colored light all over. The night they met, Chick Webb was playing, and Ella Fitzgerald was singing "A-Tisket, A-Tasket." Sometimes I can almost see them all there, doing the fox-trot and the waltz. I grew up knowing more about the music of her day than about my own. Diantha is a rock freak, but I'm not.

She cooked another batch of pancakes and poured more cocoa, and we ate till we were stuffed. Even Lilac couldn't eat any more.

Dad stood up. "Well, I'll go earn my breakfast now. You youngsters do what you want. Maybe you can help Grandma."

"That's what we came for," I said. "We're going to clean house."

And we did. For about two hours we vacuumed and dusted and took the braided rugs outside to shake them. We washed the dishes, and washed the kitchen floor and the bathroom floors. Grandma may be a bit "chaotic," as Dad said, but she likes things squeaky clean. The faucets have to shine, and the tiles in the shower stall have to be scrubbed.

I discovered something new about Lilac: If you suggested to her what needed to be done, she worked very hard and well. Grandma worked with us, but she never told us what to do. I noticed that Lilac would look at her when she had finished something, like carefully dusting all the miniature farm animals that Grandpa carved long ago, to see if Grandma approved. Grandma noticed, and made a point of praising Lilac's work.

Finally, she stopped us. "I think you've worked hard enough. Ellis, why don't you show Lilac the barn and the chickens and everything. Introduce her to Brandy and Peaches. By the time you get back, I'll have scared up a bite of lunch. And tell your dad he'd better come in now. That sun is fearfully hot. Tell him I stocked up on Diet Cokes for him, and there's some of your granddad's Canadian beer."

I gave Dad the message. He did look hot, but there was a big pile of weeds pulled up and ready for the composter. I took Lilac out to meet the chickens, and then we went into the barn. It seemed lonesome with Bess's stanchion standing empty. The floor had been swept clean, but there was still hay in the haymow, so we climbed the ladder and sat in the sweet-smelling hay, looking out the diamond-shaped window that faced east. You couldn't see the ocean but you could smell it.

Lilac lay on her stomach and gave a great sigh.

"What's the matter?" I said.

"This place is like heaven," she said. "I never saw a place like this."

I knew what she meant. "Someday I intend to live here," I said. "Maybe Jay, too. Diantha wants to live in Boston."

After a few minutes she said, "When you live here, can I come visit you?"

"You can stay as long as you want." I was certainly surprised to hear myself saying that.

She was quiet again for a while. Then she said in a sad little voice, "That's years from now."

chapter **13**

When we went back to the house, Grandma had washed up, changed into a pretty blue linen dress, and redone her hair, ready to go see Gramps. Dad was cooking hamburgers, and there were potato chips and a pitcher of milk on the table for us.

"I'll be over to see Dad," my dad said, "as soon as I feed the tribe and take them home."

"He'll be glad to see you," Grandma said. "Ellis and Lilac, thank you for all your help." She gave me a hug. Then she put her hands on Lilac's skinny shoulders. "As soon as Jack gets settled down here, I want you and Ellis to come and stay with us awhile. If you'd like to."

"I'd like to." Lilac's voice sounded squeaky.

"I'm glad you're here." Grandma leaned forward and gave Lilac a light kiss on the cheek. Lilac looked dazed.

"See you later." Grandma grabbed her purse and left. We heard the car back out of the barn and take off fast.

Dad grinned. "Ma should have gone out for the Indy 500."

We ate two hamburgers each and two glasses of milk and a piece of Grandma's lemon meringue pie. Lilac was silent.

"How'd you like Grandma?" I said.

She looked at me as if it were a silly question. "I like her."

"When it came to parents," Dad said, "I lucked out."

"I have three aunts," I told Lilac, "and they're nice, too, although Aunt Jennifer is kind of bossy."

"Where are they?" Lilac said.

"One's in Colorado, two in California."

"Did you like them?" she said to Dad.

"Oh, yeah, we get along fine. They're all older than I am, so they babied me. That's why I'm so spoiled." He chuckled. "I was spoiled rotten."

He's said that often, and Mom sometimes comes back at him with a line from some old song from her youth that goes "But oh boy, look at you now!"

When we got home, Dad left us and went to the hospital. Diantha was out with her friends, and Jay was riding. Mom was alone, reading the Sunday paper and listening to the radio.

"Did you have a nice time?" she said.

I said yes, and Lilac said, "I can't find my riding pants."

"I sent them to the cleaner," Mom said. "He'll bring them in the morning."

Lilac got her belligerent look, and I knew what she was thinking: They were *her* pants, and what right did Mom have to send them to the cleaner? But she didn't say anything. Instead, she went upstairs to her room, and I heard her door close—and probably lock.

"What do you think your grandmother thought of her?" Mom said.

"I think Grandma liked her a lot."

"Really?" Mom sounded as if that were hard to believe.

"Grandma gets inside people's heads and listens."

"What an uncomfortable figure of speech," Mom said, but she smiled. "And I don't do that, do I?"

"Well, you're busy."

"So is your grandmother. Ah, well. To each her own. I was never a howling success with children."

"You do all right with us."

"Thank you, dear." She pulled her glasses down from her forehead and began to read again.

"Lilac went to church."

That got her attention. "Church? Where?"

"St. Mary's."

"Oh, Lord."

"That was the idea."

She laughed. I was glad I'd caught her in a good mood. Some days she would have scolded me for being sacrilegious. "Well, I can't worry about that. She's only temporary."

I wished she hadn't said that. It sounded cruel, somehow.

"Why on earth doesn't she unpack her suitcase? The thing weighs a ton. I cleaned her room this morning, and I could hardly move it."

"I don't know," I said. "Mom, do you think I'm

going to get to go to the Equestrian Center? If I'm not, I have to let them know."

She chewed the bow of her glasses, thinking. "I don't know what to say, Ellis. If your grandparents feel up to keeping her, then you can go as you planned. If they don't, she would either have to depend on you or go home."

"I don't see how we can send her home. You can't bounce people around like that, even if they are only ten years old."

"I know you have your heart set on that horse place, but frankly, I wish you weren't going. It sounds like a lot of hard, dirty, dangerous work."

We'd been over all that a hundred times. "Well, I think I'll go see Maddie for a while," I said. "As long as you're here. Lilac's in her room, and she'll probably stay there for now."

Maddie and I went for a long ride. She thought I ought to go to the E.C. anyway, and let somebody else worry about Lilac. The thing is, nobody else will, except Grandma, and maybe she can't.

When I got home, Dad was back, looking happy because Granddad was going home the next day.

"That news made a new man of him," he said. "Ma's going to have trouble holding him down."

I had to call Lilac for dinner, which annoyed me. With her new watch she ought to know when it was time to come down. Her door was locked, and after I knocked, I heard a scrambling sound and a snap like a lock being shut. When she opened the door finally, I noticed her suitcase was in a different place under the bed. Maybe because Mom cleaned, or maybe Lilac had been looking at whatever was in it. "You're supposed to come to dinner without being called," I said.

I thought she'd get mad, but she only said, "I lost track of the time."

Doing what? She didn't look as if she'd been asleep. I felt cross with her, not just because I'd had to call her but because she was causing me problems, big ones. And nobody was helping me solve them.

chapter **14**

On the Fourth of July Dad took us all out for a shore dinner, and later we watched the fireworks at the county fairground. I guess Lilac had never seen anything like those fireworks before.

"We just have loud things," she said, "that scare you."

"Money going up in smoke," Dad said. But he enjoys it as much as we do.

Jay had the next day off. He asked Lilac if she'd like to go to a movie with him. "It's a horror movie," he said. "It's supposed to be really good."

I thought he could have asked me to go, too, but later he said to me, "If the guys see me, I'll never hear the end of it, but I told you I'd take her off your hands, so I'm doing it."

I was really relieved to see them go off to the movies. I let Lilac use my bike, although she still wobbled so much, I was afraid she might fall off and wreck it. I called up Maddie, and she came over in the jeep. We went to our friend's house and played tennis and talked and giggled and drank iced tea, and I tried not to think about Lilac.

On the way home Maddie said, "My mother says if you want to send Lilac over sometimes when Jay comes to work, she'll keep her for a while."

I was amazed. "How come?"

"She likes her. She says a kid that hates horses that much can't be all bad."

So the very next day Lilac went over to the Ryans' house with Jay. She seemed very pleased. She even stayed for lunch, and when she came home, she talked more than I'd ever heard her. It seemed like a weird combination, Mrs. Ryan and Lilac Kingsmith, but I guess there's no accounting for taste. She said they made cookies and drank peppermint tea and talked.

"What'd you talk about?"

"Oh, lots of stuff. She told me about Sicily, where she grew up, and about how she misses her brothers and sisters."

"Do you miss yours?"

Her face changed. "I've got only one real one, my brother Davey."

"Is he up north with your mother?"

"Of course not," she said scornfully. "I told you before. He's making something of himself."

Somebody—her mother?—must have planted that phrase in her head. "What is he making of himself?"

"He's gone to sea on a big fishing boat, up to the Banks. It's a very hard life, but he likes it. He hardly ever gets home. Someday he'll own the boat and get all the profit for himself."

I said it sounded romantic, but she gave me a look as if I were out of my mind.

Diantha was in the living room sorting out a

huge box of tapes. She heard us talking, and she said, "Ellis, everybody knows that fishing is a very hard life."

"All right," I said, "all right. What are you doing with those tapes?"

She arched her eyebrows. "They're my tapes, you know. I don't have to account for them to you. But since I'm in a good mood, I'll tell you. I'm sorting out the ones I want to take to college."

It hit me harder then than it ever had before that Diantha was really going away in September, really away and not coming back except maybe for Christmas. She had been accepted at three colleges, but she'd chosen Stanford, which was not exactly right around the corner. My stomach felt cold. Diantha drives me crazy most of the time, but she's part of where I am and who I am. In four years I'd be gone myself, and then Jay. What would happen to all of us? I was scared.

"Lilac," Diantha said. "I almost forgot, you had a letter."

Lilac looked startled. "Where is it?"

"On the hall table."

She scooted out into the hall and I heard her tearing open the envelope. I followed her, out of curiosity, and she went into the kitchen, reading while she walked. Then she stood stock-still in the middle of the kitchen for what seemed like forever. Something told me to keep my mouth shut for once. I pretended to be looking in the cookie jar, which was empty.

She balled the letter up in her fist, threw it into the trash basket, and ran upstairs. I don't think she even knew I was standing there.

When I heard her door close, I looked in the trash can. The envelope was addressed in pencil with printed letters. The postmark was the village near where Lilac came from, but there was no return address. I was dying to take the letter out and read it. I made myself go out to the barn, where I sat on an old cushion and thought. It wouldn't be like going into someone's room and reading their mail. Trash wasn't sacred. Even the garbage man could read it if he wanted to. Anybody could go to the town dump and find it and read it.

After a while I went into the house. Diantha had gone upstairs, leaving her tapes in two neatly stacked piles. I knew the tallest pile was the one she'd take with her, because the new Sting was on top, and she'd never leave that. I tried to picture her room at college. Everything would be neat and orderly.

I went into the kitchen and took the letter out of the trash. It was just one page.

Dear Daughter,

Hope you are well. Marvin and I plan to get hitched next week. It's the only way out I can see. You better get those people to adopt you. There's no life here for anybody. Be nice and keep clean so they'll let you stay. I miss you and Davey so much, I can't hardly stand it. But you're better off. Life around here is no picnic nor ever was. Davey says he will be in touch with you.

Lovingly,
Your Mother

I read it twice. Did "them" mean us? Adopt

Lilac? My mother would never let her stay. But if she couldn't go home, what would she do? It was the saddest letter I'd ever read.

When I heard her coming downstairs, I stuffed the letter in my pocket and took the trash basket out and dumped it in the big trash can. She was in the kitchen when I came back. She looked at the empty trash basket, and I had a feeling she had come down to get the letter back, but she didn't say anything.

"You want to go for a bike ride or something?" I said. "Jay's bike is here. We could go to the Dairy Queen."

She shook her head and went back upstairs. I didn't know what to do with the letter. I felt as if it were burning a hole in my jeans.

The telephone rang. It was Grandma. "Ellis, you're just the person I want to talk to. Your grandfather is feeling better, but he's mighty bored. If I come in for you in the morning, would you and Lilac like to come out here for a while? He'd love to see you, and so would I."

It seemed like a godsend. Lilac liked it at Grandma's. She wouldn't feel so sad, and there'd be a lot to keep her busy. "We'd love to," I said.

"Good. I'll pick you up around ten. Is your mother there?"

"She's at the thrift shop."

"Well, I'll talk to her later. Tell her I'll bring her some corn."

When I told Lilac, I expected enthusiasm, but she looked worried. "I'm expecting someone to call me," she said. "And I won't be here."

I knew she meant her brother. "Leave a message. Tell Mom and Diantha."

"What if they're not here?"

"We've got an answering machine. Whoever calls will know it's the right house. They can leave a message."

Before dinner I heard her ask Dad if she could add a message to the answering machine. He looked surprised. "What do you want to say?"

She had written it down, and she read it to him. "This is Lilac Kingsmith. I am not here right now. Please leave a phone number where I can reach you."

"Oh, Lilac—" My mother started to object.

Dad interrupted. "No problem. Come on in the den, and we'll do a new tape. I'll say my spiel, and you can say yours."

Mom raised her eyebrows and exchanged looks with me. But Dad paid no attention. He and Lilac went off together into the den and shut the door.

"Maybe she'd like us to move out," I said. "Maybe we're in her way."

"We must be patient," Mom said. "Let's get dinner on the table."

At dinner I said, "How come Jay and Diantha and I can't put messages on the answering tape, too?"

My father frowned. "Do you have something important to say?"

"I could think of something. Like when my friends call, I could say something like 'Please call back in twenty minutes.'"

"Do you always return in twenty minutes from wherever you are? Pass your plate, Jay."

Jay passed his plate for some of the meat loaf Mom makes when she can't think of anything else.

"Hey, that would be fun," Jay said. "I could say, 'Think polo!'"

"This is not a radio station," Diantha said.

"Not to change the subject," Mom said, meaning she intended to, "Mona Harrod sent that boy back home."

"Henry?" Jay looked shocked. "She sent Henry home? Why?"

"Her boys didn't seem to get along with him."

"Nobody gets along with her boys," Diantha said. "They are A-one pains in the"—she cleared her throat—"neck."

"I was going to take Henry to the beach," Jay said. "That's terrible, shipping him back home, like he's a size that didn't fit or something."

I looked at Lilac. She looked frightened.

"What's Henry's last name and address?" Jay said to her. "I'll write to him."

"Pelletier." Lilac's voice sounded faint. "He lives with his uncle and aunt. They keep him in the attic most of the time."

"Attic!" Several of us said that at once, like a chorus.

"They think he's a *re*tard," Lilac said.

"They ought to be horsewhipped," Jay said. "That's inhuman."

Diantha laughed. "Horsewhipping, on the other hand, is humane."

But nobody else laughed.

"I'm shocked at Mona," Dad said. "It seems so cruel to get the boy down here and then ship him back, like damaged goods."

"Oh, it's just like Mona," Mom said. "She's always taking on projects with a great flair and a lot of noise, and then weaseling out." As soon as she said it, she got a funny look on her face, and I knew she was realizing she had just cut herself off from any ideas about sending Lilac back. We were stuck till fall.

Dad looked at Lilac's strained face. "As you can see," he said, "you have nothing to worry about. We like having you here."

"And we wouldn't send you back even if we didn't," Jay said. "A promise is a promise."

She relaxed a little. I felt suicidal. It looked like the end of my August plans. My only hope was the trip to the farm. But somehow I couldn't imagine Lilac spending August there without me.

chapter 15

Granddad looked thinner and older, but considering all he had gone through, he seemed good. He was sitting in the recliner that Grandma had pulled out to the front porch, waiting for us. Grandma said he'd been driving her crazy asking her when we were coming.

Grandma had come for us, bringing Mom the first corn of the year, and a lot of nice small beets that are good cooked with the greens. She stayed a few minutes talking to Mom, but she said she didn't want to leave Granddad long because "he'll get into things that he thinks need doing."

So we climbed into Grandma's car, Lilac tugging her suitcase, me with a paper bag with clean jeans, T-shirt, toothbrush, and comb.

Lilac was wearing her jodhpurs, clean and pressed from the dry cleaner. I supposed her jeans and things were in the mysterious suitcase.

When we got out of the car at the farm, I ran up the steps to hug Grandpa. "You look great!" I said.

"You look pretty good yourself. What's new? I feel like I've been in outer space for a couple of hundred light-years. Who's that behind you?"

Lilac was hanging back, clutching her suitcase. Gramps knew who it was, of course; he was just trying to be nice to her.

"This is our new friend Lilac Kingsmith," Grandma said, putting her hand on Lilac's shoulder. "Lilac, this is my Jack."

"We call him Gramps, or Granddad or Grandpa," I said, in case Lilac thought she was supposed to call him Jack. "You can call him Mr. Worthington."

"Heck, that's too big a mouthful for a little girl," Gramps said. "Call me Gramps, Lilac. Come here and shake hands."

I didn't like the idea of her calling him Gramps. He wasn't *her* grandfather. But I couldn't very well argue with Gramps, not when he'd just had a heart attack and all.

"What you got in that great thumping suitcase?" Gramps said.

"That's none of your affair, Jack," Grandma said. "A person is entitled to some privacy." Grandma had already been turned down when she offered to help carry it.

"Oh, you women," Gramps said. "You and your secrets."

Lilac grinned, a small, shy grin that I hadn't seen before. She sure had a lot of faces.

Katharine, the calico cat, jumped into Gramps's lap. Lilac jerked backward. "This here is Katharine," Gramps said. "Katharine, say hello to Lilac. You don't need to worry about her, Lilac. She likes the whole human race."

"I never had a cat," Lilac said.

"You'll like her," Grandma said.

"When you get to know her real well," Gramps said, "she'll let you call her Kit. But first you have to establish your bona fides."

Grandma laughed. "He's talking Latin at you, Lilac. That means 'good faith.' Come on, let's take you girls up to your rooms."

I had the room that I'd always had since Diantha was old enough to refuse to share a room with me. It was a small one facing the barn and the fields. On a good day you could see the haze that told you where the sea began. Sometimes after a storm you could hear the far-off roar of the surf. There was nothing in the room but my single bed and a chest of drawers and a small bookcase full of Grandma's books. I'd read them all: *Anne of Green Gables, Tom Swift and His Flying Machine, David Copperfield,* the Episcopal prayer book, *My Friend Flicka,* and a lot more. I loved them all. Lilac's room was at the other end of the hall, the room Jay usually had. There were model airplanes hanging from the ceiling, and on the shelves were racing car models, a brass horse's head, and a bunch of books about horses, serious books about how to take care of them. On the wall a big poster of a racehorse's head filled up most of the space. I wondered how Lilac would like waking up to that.

I expected she'd ask if there was a key to the door, and at least that she'd shut herself in her room till supper. But when I came downstairs, she was already there, sitting on the front steps talking to Grandpa. I was amazed. She never talked to me unless she had to. Also, I was a little bit irked. I wanted to talk to Gramps myself. I had a million questions to ask him, about the bypass operation and what it was like in the hospital.

But I couldn't get a word in edgewise. Gramps was telling Lilac all about Bess, the cow, and how much he missed her. Lilac was asking questions like how did you get cream out of milk, and what was buttermilk. She may have grown up on a farm, but it wasn't anything like any farm I knew of if she didn't even know where cream came from.

"Doesn't your farm grow anything but potatoes?" I said.

She glanced at me as if I had interrupted a private conversation. "Not much else," she said. "A few turnips and beets."

"Yuck," I said. "I hate turnips."

Grandpa gave me a surprised look. I'm usually careful not to be rude in front of my grandparents. He said, "I'm very partial to turnip greens myself."

"Corn is my favorite vegetable," I said.

"Well, that's lucky, because we're having it for supper. And your grandmother's corned beef hash. I dreamed about her hash when I was in the hospital. Hospital food tastes like the mash I used to feed Bess."

Lilac laughed. "How do you know how that tastes?"

He grinned. "I tried it once."

"You're making it up!"

Both of them were laughing like old buddies. I

132

couldn't believe it. Personally, I didn't see anything to laugh at. I'd tasted Bess's mash myself. It wasn't all that bad, although not as good as Grandma's hash.

"They give you cold rolls at the hospital," Grandpa said. "They're so hard, you could get up a baseball game if you had a bat."

I decided if they were going to sit here and go into hysterics over dumb jokes, I'd go find Grandma. I hoped the bypass hadn't made Grandpa senile. He hadn't even asked me how my riding was going. Well, if anybody wanted to know, it wasn't going anywhere since Lilac Kingsmith blew into town. Jay was riding every day, but I was baby-sitting Lilac.

I found Grandma in the kitchen shucking corn. I sat down and helped her.

"You look sad," she said. "Is anything the matter?"

"No," I lied. "Granddad looks great, doesn't he?"

"Yes, thank goodness. Now, if he'll just be careful. The doctor said he should exercise regularly on a daily schedule that he gave him. I hope Jack doesn't do more than he should. You know how he is. He always thinks nobody else can do things right around here. Have you seen his exercise bike?"

I had. I had tried it. I thought Granddad was going to get very bored riding a bike that went nowhere.

"Your plans for the Equestrian Center," Grandma said, "they're still intact, aren't they?"

"I think so." I didn't want her to know that it depended on her. If I said I couldn't go unless Lilac stayed at the farm, she'd find some way to keep her, no matter how inconvenient.

"I'm sorry Jay isn't here, too, but it's lovely that he has a job, especially with the horses he loves," she said.

I wanted to say I loved horses, too, and I probably was hardly going to get to ride, let alone go to the Center. To tell you the truth, I was feeling very sorry for myself.

"Lilac and your grandfather seem to hit it off," she said.

"Yes. That's good." I wanted to show her the letter from Lilac's mother that was still wadded up in my pocket, but I was afraid she'd be shocked at my reading someone else's mail.

"Would you like me to slice the tomatoes?" I said.

"Yes, if you will, dear."

"These are terrific tomatoes." I slid a slice into my mouth. Grandma grows wonderful huge juicy tomatoes.

Gramps is a big talker at all times, but at supper he seemed so happy to be home, he just couldn't quit. He was full of funny stories about the hospital. To hear him, you'd never guess how much pain he must have had. Lilac hung on every word, and laughed at every joke. I couldn't figure if she really thought he was all that wonderful or if she was playing up to him for some other reason.

We had strawberry shortcake for dessert, strawberries from Grandma's garden. Grandma made the old-fashioned kind of shortcake, not sponge cake or any of those dumb things. Lilac and I had seconds.

Grandma doesn't have a dishwasher, so I

washed and Lilac dried and Grandma put away. Gramps was listening to the evening news on the radio. He had finally bought a color TV and had it sent to the house after he had his surgery. He told Dad he was afraid Grandma would be lonesome without him. But he didn't like to watch it himself. He said having all those people in his living room made him uneasy.

He went to bed early in the den, and Grandma and Lilac and I watched an old Fred Astaire–Ginger Rogers movie. Lilac seemed enthralled. She sat on the sofa with her arms around her knees, her eyes wide, never looking away from the screen.

"I like the musicals best," Grandma said during the commercial. "They don't make movies like that anymore." She laughed. "Don't I sound like an old fogey. But it's true. In movies nowadays it's all violence and sex."

"Did you see *A Trip to Bountiful?*" I said, knowing she had. I have to defend my own times, don't I?

"Yes, I did, and you're right, it was wonderful. Geraldine Page was very moving."

Lilac looked blank. I started to ask her if she'd seen it, but I didn't. I knew she hadn't, and that would be rubbing it in. She was a lot quieter with Grandma than she was with Gramps, but I could tell they felt comfortable with each other. I didn't want Grandma to think I was being mean to Lilac.

Grandma stays up till midnight usually, and this night she let us sit up, too, so we could see the end of the movie. She loved having the television, and I thought about how she had never asked for one because she knew Gramps disapproved.

Everyone took it for granted that Grandma didn't want one either. Maybe you had to be a sacrificer when you married, but I didn't think I would be, not on everything anyway. Let the man make a few sacrifices. It wouldn't kill Gramps to have a TV in the house. He didn't have to watch it.

I was thinking these things after I'd gone to bed, and suddenly I was shocked to realize that I was feeling mad at Gramps. I loved him. I never got mad at him, or hardly ever. What was the matter with me? I thought about it awhile, and all I could come up with was Lilac. It bugged me that he gave her so much attention.

Katharine, the cat, pushed my door open and jumped up on my bed. I hugged her. If you squeezed her ribs a little, it made her purrs come out in loud jerks. She nibbled my cheek. Sometimes she gets a little carried away with those love bites and it hurts, but tonight I was so glad to have her with me, I didn't care.

"You better stay away from that Lilac," I told her, "I don't think she's a cat person."

chapter 16

I slept late. It's so quiet on the farm, there's nothing
to wake you up except the rooster. He'd waked me
for a few minutes around five o'clock, but once I'd
remembered where I was, I'd gone back to sleep.

I took a shower, and while I was getting dressed
in my room, I looked out the window. Gramps and
Lilac were out in the barnyard feeding the chickens.
He was showing her how to take a handful of corn
out of the round tin basket and throw it kind of
sideways so it scattered. Surely a potato farm or any
kind of a farm would have chickens. Maybe she didn't
get to feed them. Or maybe she was pretending not
to know how so Gramps would pay attention to her.

I was usually the one who helped with the chickens. I liked to collect the eggs. It was exciting to find
them there where there hadn't been anything the
night before. They always felt so warm and smooth.
But before I even got my shirt buttoned up, Lilac
and Gramps had gone into the hen house, and in a
few minutes Lilac came out carefully carrying an

egg in each hand, and put them into the wicker basket.

The cat was lying on my bed with all four feet sticking straight up, hoping I'd scratch her stomach. "Kit," I said, "I got a feeling I'm about as necessary around here as a fifth wheel."

Of course Gramps and Lilac had had breakfast hours earlier. Grandma had another cup of coffee with me while I ate her creamy scrambled eggs on toast and drank the grapefruit juice that I can't live without. I like a special kind that comes from Texas. She never forgets.

"I've got to get caught up on my quilts," she said. "I'm way behind. The woman at the gift shop called me yesterday wanting more." She sipped her coffee. "Lilac said she could help with the piecing. Her mother used to make quilts."

"I'm sure," I said.

Grandma gave me a long look. "Lilac irks you, doesn't she?"

"I think she's an operator."

"Well, I don't know whether she is or not. But let's give her the benefit of the doubt, shall we?"

"Sure," I said. I don't think I sounded convincing.

"Jack likes her. I like her, too, as far as I know her."

"She bugs Mom." I needed some show of support.

"Your mother hates having her life disrupted. And she really wasn't braced for a strange child. She thought we'd be able to take her. Well, we'll have to see how it goes. If Jack doesn't get too tired, we might be able to have her here at least part of the time."

She began to stack the dishes.

"I'll wash." I thought I'd better make myself useful or everybody except the cat would forget I existed. What was really driving me crazy was what I should do about Mr. Blaise at the Center. Time was getting short, and it wasn't fair to wait till the last minute to cancel out. Everything seemed so uncertain.

When Granddad came in to rest, Lilac disappeared into her room. I wandered around outside, missing Jay. I got an old tennis racquet and whacked a ball against the side of the barn, but that got pretty boring. I watched the chickens awhile. The rooster was commanding his number-one hen to come and get the grasshopper he'd caught. He is a very bossy rooster, named Trumpeter. Brandy and Peaches flew up to my shoulders and let me carry them around for a few minutes.

I went into the barn and tidied up Bess's stanchion, missing her. She'd been a pretty Jersey. Cows are dumb but they're nice.

When I went into the house, Lilac was sitting on the kitchen stool and Grandma was trimming the edges of her hair.

"You should have seen it before I cut it," I said.

"You did a good job, Ellis. Just a few ragged places here and there."

She was being tactful. I wondered if that was how minorities felt when white people praised them for something they would have taken for granted in other white people. Like "Isn't it splendid that you're going to a fine college like Colby." I'd heard my mother say that once to a black girl who had done

139

some clerical work for my father. She said it as if Amanda had just gotten a Rhodes scholarship. It was patronizing, but she got mad at me when I pointed it out. So that was how I was beginning to feel, like a minority person who had to be praised out of all proportion so she wouldn't get her feelings hurt. Bull. I thought I'd call up Maddie later and see if she could come get me. Maybe we could go riding. I wasn't stuck here, after all. Gramps and Grandma could have Lilac all to themselves.

I mentioned that I might call Maddie.

"Of course," Grandma said. "I'll drive you into town if she can't come get you." She sounded relieved.

A few minutes later Lilac trailed upstairs after me. "If you go home," she said, "will you check and see if I've had any mail or telephone calls?"

"They'd let you know."

"But could you check?"

. "All right."

When I got to Maddie's, I felt as if I'd just gotten out of jail. I was glad to see her, and to see Jay, who was currying his favorite, Tempest. I was even glad to see Mrs. Ryan.

Her first and only words to me were "Where's that nice little girl?"

"How come," I said to Maddie later, "Lilac is 'that nice little girl' to everybody but me? I haul her around, take her shopping, wash her clothes, feed her when she's hungry, which is nineteen times a day, and she can't stand me. If she's faced with being alone with me, she goes to her room and locks her door."

Maddie laughed. "She's an odd one. How do the

grandparents like her?"

"Grandma is willing to believe she's a good kid; Gramps thinks she's the greatest thing since sliced bread. She tags around after him and does all the chores Jay and I usually do, talks a blue streak to him, and he eats it up."

Maddie took off her sunglasses and looked at me. We were sitting on her back steps. "Do I detect the little green imp of jealousy here?"

"Of course not," I said. "Why should I be jealous of Lilac Kingsmith, of all people?"

"I don't know," Maddie said, "but I think you are." She gave me a piece of grape bubble gum, my favorite. "I can see why, I guess. She's messed up your summer. It seems to me you're the fall guy in all this noble Christian work that Mrs. Hallowell is getting credit for in her Roman palace."

Maddie's sympathy made me feel better.

"Now that she's with your grandparents, though, I should think you could get away from her fairly often. Come over here whenever you can. Also, if your grandparents want a vacation from her, my mother would love to have her for a day."

"Why?"

Maddie thought about it. "Mama tends to see herself as a minority person. She doesn't really fit in with the Maine ladies. Lilac doesn't fit in either. I guess it's misery liking company."

When Jay came out to sit with us for a few minutes, he asked about Lilac, too. I told my story all over again, but not quite so angrily this time. I didn't want him to think it was his fault or anything. Because it wasn't.

I needn't have worried. Within two minutes he

141

had forgotten all about Lilac and was telling me how wonderful Tempest was, and Whitey, too, now that he was settling down. "Me and Mr. Ryan are going to put up jumps in the paddock tomorrow. Next time you come, you want to give it a try?"

I'd never done much jumping because I was always scared I'd hurt one of Mr. Ryan's horses. But there was nothing I'd rather do more. "Would he let me?"

"You can jump on Whitey," Maddie said. "He's a steeplechase horse."

That really cheered me up. "When will they be ready?"

"Give us a couple days." Jay offered me some cherry bubble gum and I stuffed it into my mouth, forgetting I already had a wad of grape. I popped a multiflavored bubble.

Jay saddled up two of the horses for us, and Maddie and I went for a ride on the bridle path that led through the woods. It was a perfect day, and I felt happy, one of the few times since L.K. came.

"Jay seems to be having a super time," I said.

"Yeah, he really loves the horses. My dad says he has the gift. For that matter, my brother is raving about him, too. Jay goes out there to the shed when he isn't busy, and Cy teaches him about computers. He says Jay learns faster than any adult he's ever taught."

I was glad Jay was having a good summer. He'd had a miserable school year with a teacher who picked on him because he asked too many questions that the teacher couldn't answer.

Dad was going out to the farm after work, so

when we came back from our ride, I had to go home, so as not to miss catching a lift back to the farm. Diantha was there, trying on new clothes. She was already outfitting herself for college in the fall. When it comes to clothes, Diantha thinks ahead. She made me inspect her and of course praise her in every new outfit she'd bought. She did look good in them. Diantha has a flair for clothes. I wished she weren't going away.

When she came back from one of her interminable phone calls, I said, "In two months I'll have the phone to myself. Except for Mom. What a break."

"You'll be sorry when I'm gone, gone, gone." She sang it.

"In a pig's eye I will."

"Speaking of messages and such, there's a letter for Lilac. You want to take it to her?"

"Sure." I expected it to be another bundle of joy from her mother, but it was different handwriting, with a Nova Scotia postmark. "It must be from her brother."

"Which one? She's got four or five, hasn't she?"

"Only one real one." I put the letter in my pocket.

Diantha put on a big floppy straw hat. "You like it?"

It was a crazy, dippy hat, but she looked great in it. "It's okay," I said.

"Your enthusiasm bowls me over." She took it off. "I tried to get Dad to take that crazy message of Lilac's off the answering machine, but he wouldn't. People think it's weird. That squeaky little voice and that odd name."

"Has she had any messages?"

"Of course not. Who would call her?"

Dad drove in just then, and soon after that he and I left for the farm. He asked me how things were going. I said fine. I didn't want any more comments about me being jealous.

Gramps and Grandma and Lilac were sitting on the porch drinking iced tea. Just one little happy family. I went in the house to get glasses for Dad and me. I don't really like iced tea or hot tea either, but I wasn't going to be left out.

Lilac was asking Dad if she had had any messages.

"I'm afraid not," he said. "Not so far."

Grandma looked amused, and I thought she was thinking what Diantha had said—who would call Lilac? It was kind of sad when you thought of it, to have nobody to call you. Especially when you seemed to expect it. I suddenly remembered the letter. I took it out of my pocket and gave it to her.

Her face lit up like a two-hundred-watt bulb. She ran over to the hammock to open the letter. Dad and Gramps and Grandma were talking about whether Gramps should or shouldn't get another cow, but I kept sneaking looks at Lilac. She opened the envelope very slowly, as if she were scared to look. She took out what looked, from where I sat, like a telegram. She read it carefully, frowning. Then she looked inside the envelope again and shook it, but it was empty. She studied the piece of paper again.

Dad glanced at her. "Good news, Lilac?" Lilac's family situation being what it was, it didn't seem like the most tactful thing he could have said, and I saw Grandma give him a reproachful look.

Lilac got up slowly, leaving the hammock swinging and squeaking, the way it always does. She came to my father and held out the piece of paper. "What is this?"

He looked at it. "It's a postal money order for fifty dollars, made out to you. It's signed by David L. Kingsmith."

"You're rich, Lilac," Gramps said. He meant to make her smile, but she didn't.

"There isn't any letter." She showed them the empty envelope.

"It's postmarked Nova Scotia," Dad said, "but it's a U.S. money order. You have to cash it at the post office. They'll give you fifty dollars for it." He looked at me. "Has she got any identification?"

I shrugged. How should I know? She might have reams of ID in that suitcase of hers.

"I'll take her to the village post office in the morning," Grandma said. "They'll cash it on my say-so."

"Why are you looking so sad?" Gramps said. "If somebody sent me fifty bucks, I'd turn cartwheels."

Grandma frowned and shook her head at him.

Lilac took back the money order and went into the house. You could hear the stairs creak as she ran up to her room.

They all looked at me. "It's her brother," I said. "The only one in the family she's friends with. I think she thought he was coming to get her. He's a fisherman."

"Nova Scotia," Dad said. "That figures."

"It was nice of him to send money," Grandma said, "but it would have been nicer to say something, even just 'Love from your brother.' She's such a lonely child."

"Well, Johnny, are you staying for supper?" Gramps said. "Your mother's made one of her fantastic clam chowders."

"I wish I could." Dad stood up. "I promised to go to somebody's buffet supper with Muriel. I hate buffet suppers. The food keeps sliding off your plate."

"That's because you put too much on it," Gramps said. "Let me know what you think about the cow."

Lilac didn't come down for supper. Grandma took a bowl of chowder upstairs and knocked, but there was no answer. Through the closed door she told Lilac it was outside the door. But when I went up an hour later, it was still there, cold. I took it back downstairs so the cat wouldn't eat it.

Gramps fussed about Lilac. He thought we should do something. "She's upset, poor little tyke."

"Leave her alone," Grandma said.

"It beats me how fifty dollars could upset a person," Gramps said, "but there's no accounting for tastes."

chapter **17**

Lilac didn't appear again till the next day. And then she seemed very quiet, although she helped wash the dishes and went out with Gramps to do the chores, the same as usual. Later in the morning Grandma drove her into the village and the post office cashed the money order for her. She came back with a fifty-dollar bill that she took up to her room. Gramps wanted to put it in the bank for her, but she shook her head.

"Leave her alone," Grandma said. "It's her money."

"Supposing the house burns down?" he said. "Or somebody breaks in?"

"It never has, and they never did," Grandma said.

Maddie and I had left it that she would call me when the jumps were ready. I could hardly wait. She did call, but she said they wouldn't be finished till the next day. Jay was giving them a fresh coat of white paint. I didn't say a lot to the grandparents about jumping because I knew they'd think it was dangerous. They used to do a lot of things that seemed dangerous to me, like skiing and climbing Mount Washington and running the rapids in a canoe, but they weren't horse people, and I guess people are scared by what they don't know.

The next day Maddie called to say the jumps were ready. When I found out Grandma was going to town to shop for groceries, I bummed a ride. Lilac was busy helping Gramps inspect the corn for borers, so I don't think she even knew I'd gone.

Maddie was waiting for me with her horse and Whitey all saddled. Jay had gone off somewhere with Mr. Ryan to look at a horse somebody wanted to sell.

We rode out back to the big paddock, and there they were, two beautiful clean white jumps with not even a grass stain on them.

"Dad and Jay tried them out," Maddie said, "to get the distance between them right. Dad said to remind you to lean way forward over the horse's shoulders when he jumps. Raise up a little in your stirrups and kind of go with him, if you know what I mean."

I knew what she meant all right, but I wasn't sure I'd do it properly. She took off the top rails so we could start off easy.

We cantered around the paddock for a few minutes to warm up. Then Maddie led off at the first jump. Her horse, Bravo, sailed over the first jump and then the second, clean as a whistle, with space to spare.

I took Whitey around one more time, my heart pounding. Then straight at the first jump. At the last minute he refused, and I nearly sailed over his head.

"Make him go again," Maddie called. "Keep your knees tight."

On the second try he took the jump. There was a slight clatter as his hind hooves barely touched the rail, but he didn't dislodge it. Not the greatest jump ever made, but we were over, and he took the second one perfectly. It was the most tremendous thrill, feeling him sail through the air, as if I were riding my horse across the sky. Except he came down with a jolt.

After that he got better and smoother every time, and I stopped tensing up. We were doing the routines together, in sync, like dancing. By the time we stopped, I was so happy, I could hardly stand it.

When Grandma came for me, she looked at my face and said, "Whatever you've been up to, you had a good time."

I had to tell her about it. I was too full of it to keep still. She listened, nodding.

"I think I know what you mean. I used to feel that way when I skied a fast, tricky slope. Your spirit seems to fly ahead of you. Maybe it's what they call an out-of-body experience."

I should have known she'd understand. "I'm a little bumpy in the saddle still," I said, "but Maddie says I'm getting it." I told her what Maddie said about how smart Jay was with horses and computers. She smiled.

"Your dad likes to say he lucked out with parents. His luck is nothing compared to ours in our grandchildren." She patted my hand. "We'll miss Diantha, won't we?"

"Yes. I miss her already. She's a pain, but I like her a lot. Has Lilac cheered up any?"

"She's very quiet."

I thought of telling her about the letter, but I hated to have her think I was a snoop, so I didn't.

I guess I chattered about horses all through supper. Lilac didn't even look at me. It probably wasn't tactful of me, since I knew how she felt about horses, but I couldn't keep it to myself. Gramps wasn't crazy about my jumping, but all he said was "I guess there are worse things."

"Like I could drive cars ninety miles an hour," I said. "Or I could be a crack addict, or I could be a child porn star."

He laughed. "You're right, kiddo. Stick with the horses."

Lilac didn't stay to help with the dishes. She followed Gramps out to the barn to check on the supply of hay. His mind was made up to get another cow.

"Go with them if you want to," Grandma said. "I can do these dishes up in a jiffy."

I didn't.

I met Lilac in the upstairs hall when I was getting ready to go to bed. It was early, but I was too tired for TV. She looked more cheerful than she had all day.

"Gramps is going to name the new cow Lavender," she said. "Lavender is close to Lilac, get it?"

I got it all right, and it made me mad. He'd never named a cow Ellis. Of course, that wasn't the best name in the world for a cow, but neither was Lavender. "Why not Purple?" I said. "Why not Mauve?"

She looked blank. "Are you mad because he's naming a cow for me?"

"What my grandfather names his cows," I said, "is not the most fascinating subject in the world as far as I'm concerned."

She gave me that little secret smile that I hadn't seen for some time. "You're mad because he isn't naming it for you."

"You are out of your half-baked little mind," I said. "You are getting delusions of grandeur, that's what you're getting. It's time you grew up, Lilac. You're just sulking because your mother said your brother would come see you and he didn't—" I stopped, realizing what I was saying. Her face changed. She looked pale, and then suddenly bright red with rage.

"You read my letter!" she said in a low, furious voice. "I knew it. I knew it when you rushed the trash can outside. You read my private mail. I could get you arrested."

"Why would I want to read your mail?" I tried to sound lofty, but it came out pretty feeble. I was trapped. "Anyway, stuff in trash cans is public property. Anybody can look at what's in trash cans. What do you think bag ladies do?"

"You got it all," she said, her teeth clenched. "I hate your guts."

"I hate you, too," I said.

We went to our rooms and slammed the doors. If I was going to have to give up my wonderful month in Massachusetts to baby-sit a brat who hated my guts . . . well, I just was not going to do it. That was all there was to it.

chapter **18**

I was so mad and upset, I didn't think I'd sleep all night. But maybe your unconscious wipes you out when things get too tough to face. Anyway, I went to sleep, and sometime during the night I had a weird dream. I dreamed I was wandering around this enormous, humongous palace made of stuff that looked like gold. The furniture was all beautiful velvet and satin, but everything was too big, like for giants. I couldn't even climb into one of the chairs.

Nobody was around. I walked and walked down marble corridors, looking in these beautiful rooms, and all I could hear was the sound of my bootheels. I remember I was scared they'd scar the floor. Then I came to the biggest room of all, like a ballroom, and there were people in there. People I knew, only all dressed like princes and princesses. I couldn't hear a sound, but my parents were waltzing, my dad in knee breeches and a velvet coat, my mom in something gauzy and full. Gramps and Grandma were jitterbugging, and they were all dressed up, too.

Grandma's full skirt spun around her like a silver cloud. I saw a kind of throne, and Diantha descended from it, wearing a crown and one of the dresses she'd shown me that afternoon. About twenty handsome young men appeared suddenly and danced around her. She waved a wand, and they changed positions. Off in a corner on a smaller throne Jay was asleep. He had on short velvet pants, a frilly blouse, and a little crown, like a circlet, that had slipped down over his eyebrows, the way he wears his baseball cap. I looked for myself, but I wasn't there. I was outside, and the transparent lacy curtains that were the walls of the room were made of something hard as steel. I waved and waved, but they didn't see me.

There was a large crystal chandelier hanging from the ceiling. It began to shake, as if there were an earthquake. I tried to tell them to look out. I pounded on the see-through wall, but it hurt my hands. Lilac was standing right underneath the chandelier. She was wearing her jodhpurs. I saw the chandelier break loose and fall.

I woke up sitting bolt upright, hugging the cat so hard she was trying to get loose. My heart was smashing against my ribs, and I could hardly breathe.

The whole dream had been in total silence, and now the house was silent, too. I wished I were home so I could get into bed with Diantha. She'd complain, but she'd let me in. I felt so scared.

The little digital clock that I'd brought with me said two thirty-five. Moonlight was pouring in the windows. I got up and squeezed into the little rocker I'd had when I was a child. The barn looked silvery in the moonlight, and the hen house was dark and shadowy. I tried to think what the dream meant, but it was already slipping out of my mind.

Why did Lilac hate me? I tried to think about her life. Maybe she hated me because I still had my father, and hers was dead. I still had my brother, and hers had gone away. I had a nice house and grandparents with a farm; she had an abandoned house full of bats.

It must have taken a lot of courage for her to come to spend the summer with strangers. "Make something of yourself." How would a ten-year-old know how to do that? I didn't know myself, except in a vague way. I was sorry I'd said I hated her.

I went back to bed and woke up again about the time Dad would generally be having breakfast. I decided to call him, just to feel better. But no one answered. He and Jay must already be gone, I decided, and Mom and Diantha unplugged their phones at night. Instead of a real person, I got the answering machine. Lilac's thin, childish voice said, "This is Lilac Kingsmith. I am not here right now. Please leave a phone number where I can reach you." Nobody had thought to take her message off the machine. And her brother Davey had never called, had sent fifty dollars without even a "Love, Davey." I felt as if I couldn't stand it.

I went back to my bedroom, got a yellow legal pad and a pen from the desk drawer, and I wrote:

Dear Lilac: I'm sorry I said I hate you, because I don't. I think you are very brave. I apologize for reading your mother's letter. Some trash isn't trash at all, and it's very private. I know you are worried about what will become of you. If Granddad isn't well enough for you to stay here, you can stay with us. I'll be there. Don't worry about the future. My father is very good at solving problems.

Your friend,
Ellis Worthington

I folded it and wrote her name on the outside. Then I went down the still-dark hall and stuck it under her door.

When I came down to breakfast, Lilac and Granddad were out in the barn. I said, "How is Lilac this morning?" I thought Grandma must have heard us yelling at each other the night before.

"It's hard to tell with Lilac, isn't it? She has a poker face. But I think she's all right. She and Jack are making plans for a new cow." She sighed. "I hope Jack isn't taking on too much too soon. But I might as well talk to the side of a barn. I can't hold him back, and I suppose I wouldn't want to, really." She looked at me. "I have to go to the dentist, if you'd like a ride into town."

I leaped at the chance, dying to take Whitey over the jumps again. Also I was embarrassed about seeing Lilac. Maybe the note was a mistake. She might sneer at it and not believe a word of it. Grandma dropped me off at my house. Diantha and Mom were still asleep, so I got out the cooking things and made a pan of johnnycake. It's one of the few things I can bake with some success. I left it to cool on the table with a note saying, *"From me to you because I miss you. Love, Ellis.*" I thought about Lilac's mother missing her, and how much Lilac must miss her mother and her brother.

What I didn't want to think about was what was hanging over me. I knew I ought not to go off for a whole month and leave the responsibility of Lilac to Grandma and Granddad. He wasn't well, and she looked tired. They shouldn't have that responsibility dumped on them.

On my way to Maddie's I stopped at the bookstore and bought *Pippi Longstocking* for Lilac. Maybe it was too young for her, but I still liked it myself.

At Maddie's I could forget about Lilac for a while. Whitey was feeling frisky, and I had to ride him around before I dared tackle the jumps. Jay and Cy came out to watch us both, or at least to watch Maddie, who was jumping beautifully. Cy and Jay seemed to have become good friends. Cy is shy, and I never knew him well. I was glad he liked Jay and would teach him about computers. Jay was having a good summer. I was glad somebody was.

"All right, Whitey, let's go," I said finally. I brought him around and headed for the jump, but he shied at a squirrel outside the paddock.

"He's got to learn not to do that," Maddie said. "A polo pony can't act like that."

Cy and Jay were sitting on the top rail of the paddock fence, their heels hooked over the lower rail, watching us. Jay looked tanned and taller. "You've grown," I said.

"I work out at the gym with Cy," he said. "You ought to see me pumping iron." He flexed his biceps as he jumped off the fence and came over to me. "Listen, I've decided to give you fifteen percent of my pay."

"Why?"

"Because I'm having such a good time, and you aren't."

"I am now."

"I know, but you're stuck with the potato kid, and I got out of it."

I was touched.

With that he went back to the stable, and Cy went, too. I was just as glad; it made me kind of nervous to have people watch me jump. I wasn't all that sure of myself yet.

When Maddie took the chestnut over the jumps, it was so smooth, it seemed as if they made no effort at all. I wanted to be able to do it just like that.

"All right," I said to Whitey. "Here we go." I nudged him into a quick canter, and he took the first jump like a dream. Then, as he gathered himself for the second, four blocks away a freight train whistled. Whitey shied and crashed into the second jump, and I flew over his head.

chapter **19**

I was in the hospital with my leg in traction. It was a compound fracture in two places. My mother, looking pale, stood beside my bed, Diantha right behind her. Dad was coming in the door. I was still groggy from the anaesthetic, but I looked for Jay, until I remembered he couldn't come to the hospital; too young.

"I'm too young to be here," I said. "It's against the rules."

Diantha laughed—with relief I decided—but Mom looked as if she thought I was delirious.

"Shorty," Dad said, "what have you been up to?"

"Not up enough," I said. "That was the problem." Man, that anaesthetic really makes you witty.

"How do you feel?" he said.

"With my nerve ends."

The doctor walked in the door and laughed. "All right, Ellis, cut the comedy. How do you really feel? That's an official question." He touched the guillotine-looking affair that was holding my leg suspended in air, and I gave a small scream.

"Sorry," he said. "Is it comfortable otherwise, as long as I keep my cotton-pickin' hands off?"

"If you think lying in this position is comfortable, I guess the answer is yes."

"I *knew* that jumping business was dangerous," Mom said.

"You read too much Dick Francis, Mom," Diantha said. She was trying to help me out.

The doctor made them leave after a few minutes so I could get some sleep. I thought he was crazy to think I could sleep in that position, but I did.

I had to stay in the hospital five days, and it got very, very boring. Mom and usually Diantha came in the afternoon visiting hours, and Dad came at night. They brought me flowers and candy and books, and suffered more than I did. Grandma came on the third day.

"I would have come sooner," she said, "but Jack overdid and I had to keep him in bed for a while. If I'm not right there, he gets up." She paused. "Lilac has been a great help."

"That's great. I'm glad she's there." I really meant it.

"She sent you something." She rummaged around in her bag.

"I bought her a book before the accident," I said. "I guess it's still at Maddie's house."

"Maddie mailed it to her. *Pippi Longstocking.* She loves it." She pulled a flat book out of her bag. It was one of the "Sylvia" cartoon books by Nicole Hollander. "She read the one Jack gave me for Christmas, and she kept saying she didn't get it. I told her you loved it, so she couldn't wait till we got you the new one. She paid for it herself."

There was no note or anything. Maybe she didn't hate me so much anymore. "Tell her I love it."

After Grandma had gone, I read it. Sylvia makes me laugh, but laughing jiggled the traction so I tried just to smile. Then all of a sudden I was almost crying: mostly because I couldn't go to the Equestrian Center, but partly because Lilac had done something nice for me. Fate and Whitey had broken my leg, so I'd never know whether I would have given up the Center on my own or not. I'd like to think I would have, but it's easy to be unselfish when you don't have a choice.

The next day they got me out of traction and into a cast. I had to learn to use crutches, which is not as easy as it looks. I was going to go home the next day.

Maddie wrote every day. She said when I was lying on the ground unconscious with my leg twisted under me, and everybody in a panic, her mother stood outside the paddock wringing her hands and saying, "She'll sue, she'll sue."

Just before I left, a note came from Lilac. It said:

Dear Ellis: I hope your leg don't hurt too bad. I told you horses were no good. I'm helping Grandma do her quilt. Lavender can't come till Gramps feels better.

Yours truly,
Lilac Kingsmith

When my father came to take me home, I told him about Lilac's mother not wanting her to come home, and how she'd said "Get them to adopt you."

Dad whistled between his teeth. "Holy Moses," he said, "your mother would never go for that."

"I know." I told him about reading her mother's letter when I shouldn't have, and how guilty I felt.

He shrugged. "I wouldn't say it was the world's worst sin, reading something she'd thrown away."

I told him how she'd said she hated me, and I said I hated her, and how I wrote her a note and said I was sorry.

"How'd she react to that?"

I told him about the Sylvia book and the note.

He nodded. "It's been hard on both of you. But I have a notion you'll end up good friends."

I thought that that was about the unlikeliest idea I'd ever heard of, but I didn't say so.

"I'll talk to the people who put kids in foster homes," he said.

"Some of those foster parent-people aren't very nice."

"We'll see to it that they are."

I didn't feel good about it, though. I'd heard about foster homes that worked kids like slaves.

I had to stay home a few days before I went back to the farm. Maddie came over right away, and Jay brought me my favorite kind of Häagen-Dazs and a couple of comic books. Everybody treated me like the queen of the hive. And don't think I didn't enjoy it.

It was decided that I could go back to the farm on Sunday if I was careful. How can you be anything but careful with a thousand-pound plaster cast on your leg from ankle to hip?

Grandma was bringing Lilac in to early mass,

and they were going to pick me up afterward. Mom actually got up early to cook my breakfast that morning, although Dad had offered to do it.

"Dad can make those baked eggs he does, and Mom can squeeze the orange juice, and Diantha can pour the milk," I told them, teasing.

"My eye!" Diantha said. "There are limits. I'm not getting up at dawn to pour milk."

While we were having breakfast, Mom, looking half awake, burned the bacon and said, "Can you believe it? Your grandmother actually goes to the Catholic service with Lilac. Frances Worthington, a lifelong Congregationalist!"

Dad winked at me. "I heard her say she thought it might have been interesting to be a nun."

My mother rolled her eyes. "What is the world coming to!"

"Tolerance, maybe," Dad said.

It was Jay who poured my milk. "Will you try jumping again sometime?"

"Absolutely not," Mom said.

"Sure I will," I said.

"I forbid it," Mom said.

Dad shook his head. "I think that falls into a category that we can't forbid. Ellis is old enough to make those decisions for herself."

Jay and I grinned at each other.

"I've been working with Whitey," he said, "trying to cure him of shying. That's his only problem."

"Do you know what it costs to break a leg?" Mom said.

We all laughed so hard, she had to laugh, too,

although she kept saying, "I mean it."

When Grandma and Lilac came, I found myself feeling self-conscious with Lilac and avoided looking at her. That was easy enough, because when you're in a cast, walking on crutches, you mostly just look where you're going. Dad helped me into the backseat, which took about five minutes.

Lilac was wearing a new dress I hadn't seen. Mom told her how nice she looked.

"Grandma bought it," she said.

On the way to the farm, she and Grandma brought me up to date on the news, but Lilac didn't turn around to look at me. I found out that Gramps was feeling better and had promised to slow down a little. The cow would be postponed for a while. The corn was doing fine, and the horticultural beans (my favorite) were ready. Gramps had bought a couple of floppy-eared rabbits. "Both male, we hope," Grandma said. One of the banties had died.

When we drove into the yard, I felt as if I'd been away for years; it must be, I decided, a little like going back when you're grown-up to a place where you lived as a child. Not that I felt grown-up, only different.

Lilac held the door, and Grandma helped me out of the car and gave me my crutches. I was still very awkward with them. Gramps came out and pointed to the flagpole where he puts up a big flag on the Fourth of July and Veterans Day. The flag was flapping in the wind.

"For you," he said. "Welcome home, soldier."

Steps were still hard for me, so Grandma stood behind to brace me and Gramps stood ready to catch me if I tripped. Lilac was looking at the autographs on my cast.

"You can sign it, too," I said.

We had an early lunch. We all talked a blue streak, except for Lilac, and even she said more than usual, sometimes directly to me. Like she said the rabbits were named Johnny and Jay, and Gramps was going to buy another banty.

"He might name it Ellis," she said.

Later I decided I needed to lie down awhile and maybe read. I was really tired. Lilac came up the stairs behind me, watching every awkward move I made. Over my shoulder, I thanked her for Sylvia.

"I don't get most of those jokes," she said, "except the cat jokes."

"Maybe you have to get used to Sylvia," I said. I lay down, trying to get the heavy cast in the least uncomfortable position. It itched like crazy. "Will you do me a favor?"

"What?"

"I have to write a letter. Will you bring me the pad of stationery that's in the top right drawer? And a pen."

She got them for me and sat watching. I wished she'd go away.

"Who are you writing to?" she said.

"A man named Mr. Blaise. I have to tell him I broke my leg and I can't come to this place he has in Massachusetts."

"The horse place."

"Yes."

"Grandma told me about it. She said if they weren't able to keep me here all summer, you were

164

going to give up your horse place and look after me. Is that true?"

I shrugged. "It's beside the point. I can't go with a broken leg."

She looked at me for a long time, but she didn't say any more. After a while she got up and went to her own room. I finished the letter, the hardest one I ever wrote. I cried.

When I got up, Lilac came out in the hall and asked me to come into her room. She had never done that before. It looked very neat, clothes hung up or put in drawers. *Pippi Longstocking* was on the table by her bed.

She hauled her suitcase out from under her bed and heaved it onto the bed. Then she pulled the little wicker chair up to the bed and told me to sit down. I couldn't imagine what she was up to. I watched as she took the rope off the suitcase, took a key out of her bureau drawer, and unlocked the lock on the suitcase.

"As long as you can't do much, I thought you might like to look at what I got here. Might pass the time. Help yourself." She turned quickly and left the room.

I stared at the suitcase that had baffled me for so long, almost scared to open it. I thought of Pandora's box. But I had to look. After all, she had said to.

I turned back the cover. Inside, there were a lot of packages, all neatly wrapped in old newspapers and tied with string. I took out the one on top and opened it. It felt really eerie to be doing this. Under the paper was a copy of *A Child's Garden of Verses*.

I opened it. On the flyleaf were these words in black ink: *For my dear little daughter Lilac on her third birthday from her father, Daniel E. Kingsmith.*

You could tell the book had been read a lot. I looked through it, remembering a lot of the poems from my own childhood. As I wrapped it and put it aside, I noticed for the first time a fifty-dollar bill and a ten and four ones pinned to the suitcase pocket with safety pins. No one could call Lilac a spendthrift with her own money. But she'd used six dollars of it for me.

There was a copy of *Oliver Twist* with an inscription that said: *For Lilac on her fifth birthday, Love, Dad and Mother.*

Those were the only books, except a small black leather-bound New Testament, a photograph album, and a Bates College annual for 1965. I looked through the annual and found a class picture of a man who looked very young. "Daniel Kingsmith," the caption said, and then "Danny the Dreamer, Maine's next novelist."

In the other smaller packages there were a baseball cap with a big *B* on the visor; Lilac's birth certificate and certificate of confirmation in St. Joseph's Catholic Church; a framed enlarged snapshot, faded, of a young woman smiling into the sun. On the back of the picture someone had printed in pencil: MOTHER, DAY BEFORE SHE GOT MARRIED.

I opened the photograph album. The snapshots looked like the kind I take, usually out of focus or off center. They were neatly labeled. DANIEL AND MARIE, AT SEBAGO. There was a blur of water and the outline of a canoe in the background. There were many pictures of Lilac from infancy until the age of about six. And there were pictures of David, and some of David and Lilac together. He looked like her, only a lot bigger. There were four fairly big rocks carefully wrapped and labeled: GRANITE FROM OLD MAN OF THE MOUNTAIN; SHALE WITH FOSSIL IMPRINT; ROCK WITH MICA; MARINE FOSSILS FROM MOUNT KATAHDIN. I wondered who had been interested in geology.

As I wrapped everything up and put it all back the way it had been, I felt strange, as if I had just held other people's lives in my hands, at least one of those people four years dead. Danny the dreamer, future novelist. It made me feel very, very strange. But it also made me understand Lilac. To lose a father like that was awful.

chapter 20

Dad was coming to supper by himself. It was near the end of August, a very different August from the one I had planned. I knew from the way Grandma acted that we were about to have some kind of special occasion. I asked her, but she said Dad wanted to tell us himself.

I was sure he had found a foster home for Lilac, and I was feeling very upset. I didn't want her to go into some strange home with strange people. She'd suffered enough.

After she let me look in her suitcase that day, I told her I was very happy that she trusted me that much. When she didn't say anything, I said, "I hope we're friends now."

She nodded and said, "I have to go get the eggs."

But she had acted differently with me ever since. She talked to me, even if it was only about the new banty or what had gotten into the pole beans or what was for supper. She didn't lock herself away in her room so much, and I didn't mind anymore that

Gramps made such a pet of her. Actually, in spite of my broken leg I had had a pretty good summer, and it was partly because of Lilac.

The day before, my cast had come off, and Grandma and Granddad had taken Lilac and Jay and me for a shore dinner. We had a very nice time eating clams and lobsters with those big bibs around our necks. Granddad held his bib up to his eyes and pretended to be a bandit.

Jay said, "That reminds me, Mr. Ryan's got a new sorrel named Bandit. When you can handle it, you can try him. He's supposed to be a super jumper."

"Great," I said. "I'll ride him."

Jay grinned. "Mrs. Ryan said you'd never get on a horse again."

"I got news for her."

It was a good evening, and several times I heard Lilac laugh right out loud. It made me feel good. But there was still that anxious look in her eyes, and I knew she was worried sick about what would become of her now that the summer was nearly over. I worried about it myself.

When Dad came, he was looking both serious and pleased. I wasn't sure how to read it. We were all on the porch before supper.

"Ellis, I've got a piece of news for you."

I hadn't been expecting anything about me.

"I had a phone call from Henry Blaise. He was real sorry about your leg." He paused. "He wanted to know if you could come with Maddie and her father—you and your brother both—to spend a few days during the Rolex events and that other thing—"

"The Katherine B. Clarke Welcome Stakes," I said, not really believing what I was hearing.

"That's it. He has a spare cottage you all can have, for however long Mr. Ryan can stay away. I told him I thought you'd like to come."

"*Like* to!" I said.

Dad grinned. "That's what I told him. He says you can come for your month next year if you still want to. Sounds like a real nice guy."

I was so happy, I hardly heard what anybody said for several minutes. Then I heard Dad say, "I have something I want to talk to all of you about. Lilac especially."

She winced, and her face tightened up the way it had when she first came to us. "I know," she said, "I can't hang around here much longer."

Dad looked at his parents. "We've been talking, Lilac. We didn't consult you before because we wanted to get it settled before we asked you, to be sure there were no hitches."

I wanted to say "Get to it! Tell us."

"Myself, I'd like to keep you at our house permanently, but it wouldn't be fair to my wife, even though she has grown to like you very much."

"I'll bet," Lilac said under her breath.

"She has. She admires guts. But she's not a great hand at running a house and cooking meals and all that, and it isn't fair to add another child."

"You don't have to explain," Lilac said. "I got plans."

"What plans?" Gramps said.

She turned her head away with a kind of blind look. She could lie to us, but not to Gramps.

"The plan we worked out," Dad said, "you can take it or leave it, it's up to you. My parents would like you to stay here."

Her head jerked up, and she stared at him.

"There's a bus to the consolidated school that you can catch out on the highway. It's about a half-mile walk. It'll be cold and plenty of snow in winter, but I used to do it and it didn't kill me."

I held my breath. Lilac blinked as if the sun were in her eyes. "Will you say that again? The part about staying here."

"We want you to stay with us, Lilac," Grandma said.

"Shoot, I can't handle those hens without you," Gramps said.

"I got in touch with your mother," Dad said. "We have her permission."

Lilac looked at me.

"Do it," I said. "Go for it, Lilac."

"I'd work hard," she said in a low voice.

"Honey, nobody asks you to work hard. We know you'll do your share. They're asking you to stay because they're fond of you," Dad said.

"It would cost you money, feeding me and everything."

"Lilac," Gramps said, "we're not rich, but we can always feed one more."

"I'll give you the same allowance I give Ellis and Jay," Dad said. "That'll keep you in chocolate bars."

"You can have the money my brother sent," Lilac said to Gramps.

"We'll put that in the bank in your account."

"Does Jay want me to stay?"

"Sure he does," Dad said. I didn't know if he did or not. "And you know what Diantha said? She said, 'Oh, good, I'll have another kid sister.'"

"You're making it up."

"No, it's all true."

"Listen," I said. "I can use a kid sister myself. Someone to boss around the way Di bosses me."

Suddenly Lilac grinned, a wide, open grin. "Try it!" she said. Then she looked at Dad. "I accept."

Granddad blew out his cheeks and said, "Well, for pete's sake, let's break out the chocolate chip cookies and celebrate."

"Before supper?" Grandma said.

"Why not? It's an occasion."

So we sat on the porch spoiling our appetite for supper with chocolate chip cookies, which Granddad wasn't supposed to eat.

After a while Lilac said, "I'd better check on the new banty. She was hiding this afternoon. I think she's scared."

"Tell her everything's copacetic," Granddad said.

We watched Lilac run out to the hen house.

After a while Granddad said, "Well, shoot, Ellis, what shall we name the new banty?"

"Well, shoot, Granddad," I said, "name her Lilac."